Marcia Willett's early life was devoted to the ballet, but her dreams of becoming a ballerina ended when she grew out of the classical proportions required. She had always loved books, and a family crisis made her take up a new career as a novelist – a decision she never regretted.

She lived in a beautiful and wild part of Devon, and her surroundings inspired many of her novels.

Marcia passed away in June 2022 after a period of ill health. She leaves behind a son and two grandchildren. *Christmas at The Keep* is her last book.

www.penguin.co.uk

Also by Marcia Willett

FORGOTTEN LAUGHTER
A WEEK IN WINTER
WINNING THROUGH
HOLDING ON
LOOKING FORWARD
SECOND TIME AROUND
STARTING OVER
HATTIE'S MILL
THE COURTYARD
THEA'S PARROT
THOSE WHO SERVE
THE DIPPER
THE CHILDREN'S HOUR
THE BIRDCAGE
THE GOLDEN CUP
ECHOES OF THE DANCE
MEMORIES OF THE STORM
THE WAY WE WERE
THE PRODIGAL WIFE
THE SUMMER HOUSE
THE CHRISTMAS ANGEL
THE SEA GARDEN
POSTCARDS FROM THE PAST
INDIAN SUMMER
SUMMER ON THE RIVER
THE SONGBIRD
SEVEN DAYS IN SUMMER
HOMECOMINGS
REFLECTIONS
THE GARDEN HOUSE
STARRY, STARRY NIGHT

For more information on Marcia Willett and her books, see her website at www.marciawillett.co.uk

CHRISTMAS AT THE KEEP

AND OTHER STORIES

MARCIA WILLETT

PENGUIN BOOKS

TRANSWORLD PUBLISHERS
Penguin Random House, One Embassy Gardens,
8 Viaduct Gardens, London SW11 7BW
www.penguin.co.uk

Transworld is part of the Penguin Random House group of companies whose addresses can be found at global.penguinrandomhouse.com

First published in Great Britain as
CHRISTMAS AT THE KEEP in 2022 by Bantam Press
an imprint of Transworld Publishers
Penguin paperback edition published as
CHRISTMAS AT THE KEEP AND OTHER STORIES 2024

The stories *Ghosts*, *The Colonials*, *Kath*, *Elizabeth Drake*, *The Hawk*, *Smoke Screen* and *Daisy Miller* have all been previously published but have never appeared in the same publication before now.

A CIP catalogue record for this book is available from the British Library.

ISBN 9781804994900

Typeset in 13.25/18.5pt Fournier MT Pro by Jouve (UK), Milton Keynes.
Printed and bound in Great Britain by Clays Ltd, Elcograf S.p.A.

The authorized representative in the EEA is Penguin Random House Ireland, Morrison Chambers, 32 Nassau Street, Dublin D02 YH68.

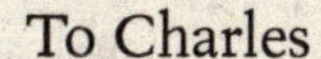
To Charles

THE CHADWICK FAMILY TREE

Edward Chadwick
1788–1881
m: 1847
Elizabeth ?
1826–1887

James Chadwick
1848–1916
m: 1886
Charlotte Bridges
1868–1897

Bertram Chadwick
1891–1916
m: 1914
Frederica Stanbury
(Freddy)
1894–1980

Peter Chadwick
1916–1957
m: 1940
Alison Pickford
1918–1957

James Chadwick
1944–1957

Felicia Chadwick
(Fliss)
1946–
m: 1970
Miles Harrington
1931–1997

Sam Chadwick
(Mole)
1952–1994
m:
Samantha Layton
1974–1998

James Harrington
1973–

Elizabeth Harrington
(Bess)
1973–
m: 1995
Matthew Foster

Sam Chadwick
1995–

Paula Foster
1997–

Timmy Foster
2002–

NOTES:

Maria Chadwick marries Adam Wishart (1948–2006) in 1995 following her divorce from Henry Chadwick.

Henry (Hal) Chadwick and Felicia (Fliss) Harrington marry in 1998.

Full details may be found in The Chadwick Trilogy: *Looking Forward*, *Holding On* and *Winning Through*, and also in *The Prodigal Wife*.

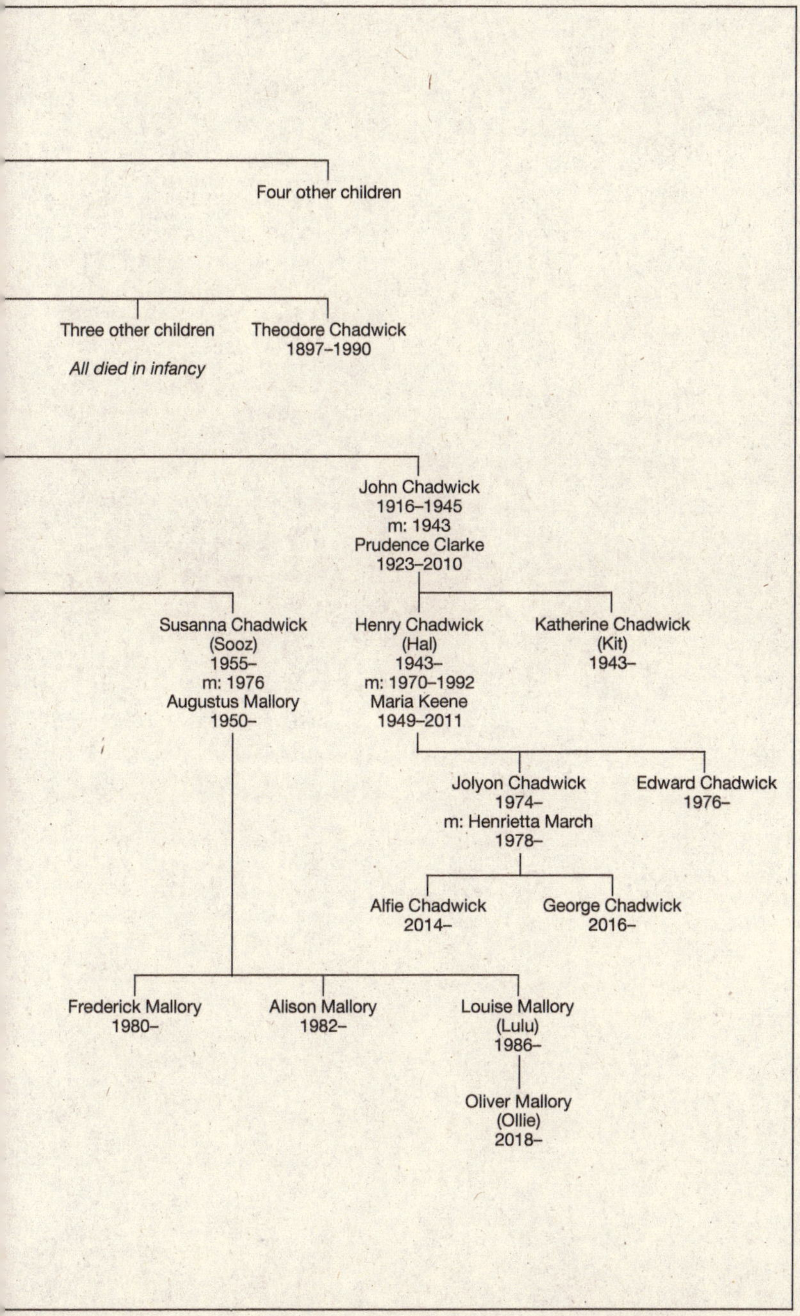

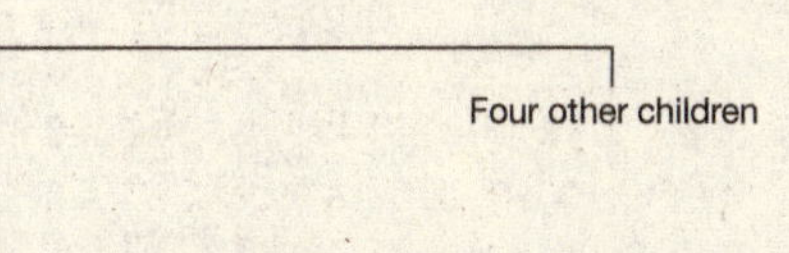

Four other children

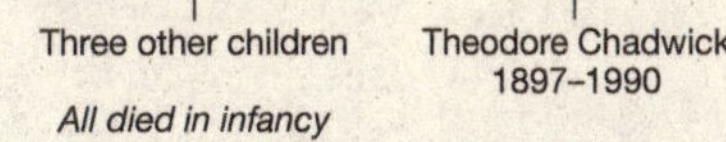

Three other children

All died in infancy

Theodore Chadwick
1897–1990

John Chadwick
1916–1945
m: 1943
Prudence Clarke
1923–2010

Susanna Chadwick
(Sooz)
1955–
m: 1976
Augustus Mallory
1950–

Henry Chadwick
(Hal)
1943–
m: 1970–1992
Maria Keene
1949–2011

Katherine Chadwick
(Kit)
1943–

Jolyon Chadwick
1974–
m: Henrietta March
1978–

Edward Chadwick
1976–

Alfie Chadwick
2014–

George Chadwick
2016–

Frederick Mallory
1980–

Alison Mallory
1982–

Louise Mallory
(Lulu)
1986–

Oliver Mallory
(Ollie)
2018–

CONTENTS

CHRISTMAS AT THE KEEP

CHAPTER ONE

October

'Ed's coming home.'

There is a little silence. Hal Chadwick puts his iPhone on the kitchen table and looks at Fliss. Ed, the black sheep of the family, Hal's younger son, who has been away in the US for ten years: it has all the makings of the return of the prodigal son. Hal picks up his phone, reads the message again and then puts the phone in his pocket. How complicated family relationships can be, especially in this particular case. Fliss is not only his second wife but also his cousin; they married when her husband, Miles, died. Hal and Maria had been divorced for several years by then and he brought their two sons, Jolyon and Edward, to the marriage, while Fliss brought her twin son and daughter. The Chadwicks are a close-knit family. Their home, The Keep, a castellated stone tower in the Devon countryside, has been there for all of them at one time or another, and now Hal and Fliss are the custodians.

Fliss is watching him. 'When you say "coming home",' she says, 'do you mean to England or here?'

Hal grimaces. 'Things haven't gone well in New York. He and Rebecca have split up.

Apparently, he's applied for a job in London, but meanwhile he says he'd like to come to see us all. He's been jabbed but he's self-isolating, of course. I'm not sure that he's got anywhere else to go.'

'Well, why not?' says Fliss lightly. 'It will be good to see him.'

Hal pushes the kettle on to the hotplate of the Aga. Since Fliss's niece Lulu and nephew Freddie are both temporarily lodged at The Keep, it would be difficult for her to refuse. And why should she? Ed has always made waves, but it seems unlikely that he will turn up now and cause trouble. Nevertheless, Hal feels a twinge of anxiety. His younger son has a clever way of exposing weaknesses, poking fun, and he hopes that Ed will behave himself.

'Is it to be a long stay?' Fliss is asking, spooning coffee into the cafetiere.

Hal shrugs. 'No idea. You know Ed. Never

quite sure what's happening next. I don't suppose he's changed.'

'You don't suppose who's changed?' Freddie appears in the doorway, a golden Labrador at his heels. 'It's quite chilly up on the hill this morning. Am I in time for coffee?'

'You certainly are.'

As a retired admiral of the fleet, Hal has a lot of respect for Freddie, whose commission as a naval chaplain has just ended. Freddie is debating his future, not certain whether to return to parish ministry or to try a different kind of chaplaincy, and he's been welcomed at The Keep whilst he deliberates.

'Here we are, Honey.' Fliss is filling the dog's water bowl. 'Drink up and you shall have a biscuit.'

Freddie sits down at the refectory table. 'So who hasn't changed?' he repeats.

'Ed's coming for a visit.' It's Fliss who answers

him. 'He's moving back and he's applied for a job in London.'

'On his own?' asks Freddie, reaching for his mug of coffee. 'Thanks, Hal. Has he split with his partner? I've forgotten her name.'

'Rebecca,' Hal reminds him. 'It seems so.'

There's a little silence, except for the sound of Honey lapping water. Nobody speaks but each imagines that the others, too, are thinking about Lulu, whose partner has recently left her and their small son, Oliver, and who, like Freddie, has taken refuge at The Keep.

'Well,' says Freddie cheerfully, 'it looks like it will definitely be a family Christmas, then.'

'Oh, no,' groans Hal. 'Please. Not the C-word. No offence, Freddie.'

Freddie grins at him. 'None taken. A thousand parish priests will be thinking the same thing. Let's just hope we don't have another Covid spike.'

'Don't even think about it,' says Fliss firmly. 'It would be so good to see everyone. The Keep packed, just like in the old days.'

'So just to be clear, Freddie,' says Hal, 'you're not leaving till next year, OK? If it's going to be that sort of Christmas, I shall need your moral support.'

'Aye aye, sir,' says Freddie, grinning at him. 'Suits me.'

'Good man,' says Hal. 'More coffee?'

Fliss watches them. She loves having Freddie and Lulu here. Her sister, Susanna, Freddie and Lulu's mother, was embarrassed when the subject of Freddie's leaving the navy first arose. Freddie would no longer have naval accommodation, and unless he got a place in a parish with a vicarage, he'd have nowhere to live. Fliss was adamant.

'Don't be silly, Sooz,' she said. 'You and Gus

haven't got that much space, and Freddie doesn't want to rush into a job just to have a house. That would be crazy, with The Keep just down the lane, and it will be lovely for us to have him. Hal's doing that deaf, grumpy-old-man thing and he's so much better with other people around.'

'You've already got Lulu and Ollie,' Sooz reminded her.

'That's different,' said Fliss. 'It was the perfect solution when the wretched Mark disappeared. And we can all help Lulu with childcare. Anyway, it would be so good for her and Freddie to spend time together. We've hardly seen him for these last five years.'

'It would be great if he could come to you,' Sooz admitted. 'He could rent something, of course, but he's been on his own so much . . .'

'If he'd be happy to be with us we'd love it,'

said Fliss. 'The Keep belongs to all of us, remember, not just me and Hal.'

'Thank goodness we're not still in lockdown,' said Sooz. 'It'll be lovely to have him here for a little while. He's been at sea so much.'

And so it was decided.

Now, Fliss wonders how the dynamic might change with Ed's arrival. She's very fond of his older brother, Jolyon, but Ed was always the tricky one. It's difficult to believe that he's been in the US for ten years, with only a few visits home, and she wonders how he'll like being back. It's strange that these three younger members of the family should all be here at turning points in their lives, and she hopes that she and Hal can help them.

She takes her mug of coffee and sits down in the rocking chair. As usual in moments of stress, she is comforted by familiar things: the long, built-in dresser with its load of pretty china and family bric-a-brac; Honey asleep in the dog basket surrounded by her toys; the warmth from the Aga. Here, more than sixty years ago, she came with Susanna and their brother, Sam, to take refuge with their grandmother after their parents and older brother were murdered by Mau Mau in Kenya. The Keep was a sanctuary for them, the family nourished them, and now Fliss draws strength from it.

CHAPTER TWO

'Ed's coming home,' Freddie says to Lulu.

He's been looking for his sister, to share the news with her, and finds her in the kitchen garden rooting up the withered runner beans and taking out the sticks. Summer is over and the harvest gathered, but with its high sheltering stone walls, and warm earthy vegetative scents, this is a good place to be in the autumn sunshine. Lulu's reaction to his news is a kind of puzzled indifference.

'Ed?' she says, resting on her fork, almost as if she's trying to remember who he is. 'We haven't seen him since he came over for his mum's funeral, have we? Has Rebecca been transferred back to the London office?'

'He's coming here. He and Rebecca have split up. Ed's applied for a job in London but he's coming down to stay for a while.'

'Split up?' She looks distressed. 'Poor old Ed. Seems to be running in the family.'

'Perhaps it's Ed that's doing the walking,' says Freddie.

He's a little surprised by his own reaction to the news: a kind of irritation that Ed is coming to disturb the peaceful tenor of things. Yet why should he assume that Ed will do that? Lulu is clearly unmoved by the situation, which makes him feel slightly guilty. Lulu glances at him, sensing his mood.

'Come on,' she says. 'I know he digs at you

for being a priest but that's just Ed. He's harmless really.'

Freddie wants to remind her of Ed's shortcomings – his experimenting with drugs at university, his inability to hold down a job for very long, the way he invested his mother's savings in a dodgy deal and lost the lot – but he resists. He doesn't want to feel like this about Ed and can't quite analyse his reaction. Perhaps it's to do with his own uncertainty at the moment: this lack of knowing where he should go next or what he should do. He seems to have lost his sense of spiritual direction and it worries him.

Lulu is watching him. 'Are Hal and Fliss OK about it? Mum used to say that Ed could be a bit of a problem.'

'I think so.' Freddie pulls himself together and smiles. 'Let's just say that I'm glad I'm in the gatehouse.'

She laughs. 'You can always escape if things get tricky. I wonder how Ollie will like him. Can you bring the bean sticks? I'll need to clean them off or they'll rot. I'll just chuck the vines on the compost.'

She kicks some mud from her boots and they walk back to the greenhouse together.

'It must be nearly lunchtime,' she says, wiping the fork tines with some leaves, then changing into her shoes. 'Shall we go and make a sandwich?'

'Fliss and Hal are meeting friends at the Cott for lunch,' he tells her. 'I thought we might have a little jaunt.'

She smiles at the family expression. 'Where do you have in mind?'

'How about Buckfast?' he asks rather diffidently. 'We could have a bowl of soup in the refectory and then a little wander round the abbey.'

To his relief, she nods. 'That sounds good.'

'We'll take my car,' he says.

As they drive through the narrow lanes between high grassy banks, Lulu thinks about Ed and wonders if the break-up between him and Rebecca has hurt him very much. She still feels the pain of Mark's leaving, unable to forget the things he said to her. He always accused her of being childish. 'Grow up, Lu!' he'd say. 'For Chrissake, you're thirty-five, not fifteen!' Hurtful things, which now she believes were a cover-up for the fact that he was having an affair; to give himself an excuse for betraying her. She knows she's not particularly clever – her elder sister, Alison, is the clever one – and his remarks are still painful to remember.

Through a gateway she glimpses the distant hills of Dartmoor, honey-coloured in the afternoon sunshine. The leaves are beginning to turn, ochre and gold and brown, and the rowan berries glow a bright red. Lulu gives a little sigh, wondering, like Fliss, if Ed will change the dynamic at The Keep. Since Covid closed down the photographic studio in Totnes for a few months she's had very little work and there's something comforting about being at The Keep with Hal and Fliss, and even more so now that Freddie has joined them.

They drive through the abbey's gateway, Freddie parks the car and they walk into the grounds towards the refectory. It's quiet today and they put on their masks, queue at the food bar for soup and rolls, then carry the trays into the refectory to find a table. They chat companionably as they eat: about their father's approaching birthday, Ollie's progress at school. At times like these the pain of betrayal recedes slightly and Lulu can feel at peace.

In the abbey, she lets Freddie precede her as

he walks slowly along the aisle beside the Stations of the Cross, studying each image, and then pauses outside the chapel to look at the amazing east window. She wonders how much he minds that his few attempts at relationships have never worked out. 'Women don't always get on with God,' he said wryly. 'And being at sea for months on end doesn't work either.'

Further on, Freddie pauses by the shelf where the candles, some already lit, stand in rows below a crucifix and she watches as he takes a taper, holds it to a flame and then lights a candle. He replaces the taper and stands quite still, his hands folded, head bowed. Presently he crosses himself, turns to look for her and smiles, and she knows as they walk back together to the car that he too has found a moment of peace.

CHAPTER THREE

Ollie waves goodbye to his friends, climbs on to his bicycle and wobbles away down the lane. He glances back to make certain that Mummy and Uncle Freddie are not too far behind, and then pushes on, singing at the top of his voice. He likes it when Uncle Freddie comes to meet him from school. It's a bit like having Daddy there. It's difficult trying to explain to his friends why his Daddy is never around. Ollie has told them that he's had to go a long way off because of his work, but his friends are a bit puzzled that Ollie never goes to visit him. But now Uncle Freddie is here and he often brings Ollie to school or meets him afterwards.

It's nice being at The Keep, too, because there's no main road so he can ride his bicycle all the way along the lane, to and from school, unless it's pouring with rain. And now a new person is coming to stay. Ed's coming home. Ollie is slightly confused about who Ed is. He knows he's Uncle Jolyon's brother but he's not quite sure why he's coming home from America. Maybe he'll bring really good presents.

Ollie's legs are getting tired. A flock of sheep jostle at a farm gate, their small, sharp hoofs slicing the turf. They watch him inquisitively and then suddenly dash away into the field. He stops cycling, the stabilizers keeping the bike steady, and he looks around.

Mummy waves. 'Nearly there,' she shouts. 'Chocolate brownies for tea,' and he nods and sets off again.

'It's nice, isn't it,' says Lulu as they follow him, 'that we're keeping up tradition. Fourth generation at the village school. D'you remember the Nativity plays?'

Freddie laughs. 'Who could forget them? I remember our dear sister dressed up as Herod and frightening the innkeeper so much he burst into tears.'

'She can still do that to me,' admits Lulu. Unbidden, a jibe of Mark's comes to mind. '"Brilliant sister. Do-no-wrong brother." You're the child of the cul-de-sac who never grows up, Lulu.' It was as if he were quoting something but she didn't ask, just in case it caused another cutting remark.

'Have you thought about school chaplaincy?'

she asks Freddie quickly, more to distract herself than to seek information.

'I've thought about everything,' answers Freddie, rather bitterly. 'These days school chaplains are required to teach, which means I'd have to train first.'

Lulu is silent, wishing she hadn't asked the question. Freddie has always been a private person, rarely sharing his feelings or plans, but she knows that he's finding it hard to adjust and wishes she could help him more. She tries to think of something helpful or positive to say, but everything she thinks of sounds banal or naïve.

Ollie gives a shout – 'Car coming!' – and climbs off his bike, dragging it into the grass verge. Instinctively they both hurry forward, as if ready to protect him, and the moment passes.

Fliss and Susanna are meeting in Bayards Kitchen at the Dartington Cider Press for tea.

'So,' says Susanna, as they sit at the table by the window, 'Ed's coming home. What's all that about?'

Fliss gives a little shake of the head, makes a face. 'Who can tell with Ed? He and Rebecca have split up and he's back from New York. He wants to come and stay for a while. Or until he gets a job.'

'Is Hal OK with that?'

'I think so.' Fliss hesitates. 'You can't always know with Hal. He's never been as close to Ed as he is to Jolyon; Ed was always Maria's boy.'

'Until he invested all her money and lost it,' says Susanna.

'Yes, well,' Fliss sips her tea, 'that certainly wasn't his finest moment, but Hal can't refuse him on those grounds.'

'And not while he's giving shelter to two of my children,' Susanna reminds her. 'I wonder how they'll all get on together. He and Freddie always managed to rub each other up the wrong way when they were younger.'

'Don't,' says Fliss. 'I'm getting too old for family conflict.'

Sooz laughs, glances down the length of the café towards the entrance and gives a groan.

'What?' says Fliss, glancing round. 'Oh, no. Clarissa. That's all we need.'

A tall woman has come in. Her grey hair is bleached an unbecoming blonde and her discontented mouth is bright with lipstick. She catches sight of the sisters and waves enthusiastically.

'Damn,' mutters Fliss, waving back, smiling brightly. 'Get ready for the third degree.'

'Looks like she's on her own,' says Sooz. 'I wonder where Ralph is.'

Fliss snorts. 'Don't ask.'

'Really?' Sooz is amused. 'Is he still . . .?'

'Yes. Ssh.'

Clarissa stops at the counter to order and

then advances up the steps, pulls out a chair, and sits down without waiting to be invited to join them.

'Well, this is good,' she announces, taking off her mask. 'I haven't seen either of you for ages. How's everybody? How's poor Lulu? What a terrible thing. So humiliating, Mark just going off like that. She must be distraught. And poor little Ollie.'

'Oh, we're all coping,' says Fliss quickly. 'How about you? Where's Ralph?'

Clarissa shrugs resentfully. 'He's at one of his meetings. Always some new charity or committee. I tell him if he'd spend half his energy in the garden or the house it would be much more useful. I thought he'd go mad during lockdown.'

The sisters attempt to look sympathetic, suppressing smiles as they swallow their tea.

'It must have been tough for him,' agrees

Sooz, 'not being able to get on with all his good works.'

'He was impossible. Grumpy, sulky. Like a spoilt child.'

Clarissa leans aside as her tea is set in front of her and mutters a thank you. Sooz glances at Fliss, a little nod, and the sisters push back their chairs.

'Got to dash,' Sooz says. 'Sorry, Clarissa. We're meeting Ollie from school.'

'Both of you?' demands Clarissa crossly, disappointed by their defection.

Fliss nods, makes an apologetic face. 'We must make a plan to have a catch-up. Love to Ralph.'

The sisters hurry out, and Fliss bursts out laughing. 'I've never heard adultery called "good works" before,' she says.

'Couldn't resist,' grins Sooz.

'And what's this about meeting Ollie from

school? Lulu and Freddie went to get him half an hour ago.'

'I know,' says Sooz guiltily. 'But I just couldn't cope with all those toxic questions under the guise of sympathy. Awful woman. I must say I don't blame Ralph. Imagine being in lockdown with Clarissa!'

They laugh as they walk up the slope to the car park.

'Why don't you come back?' asks Fliss. 'You can watch Ollie having his tea.'

'I might do that,' says Sooz. 'Gus won't be back from Exeter yet.'

Fliss raises her eyebrows. '"Good works"?'

Sooz laughs. 'He should be so lucky! He's gone to Exeter to buy a new laptop.'

'That's what he told you,' says Fliss. 'But can we trust him?'

'Gus is much too lazy,' grins Sooz. 'Choir rehearsal is quite enough. Good works would completely finish him off. See you in a minute.'

They climb into their respective cars and drive away towards The Keep.

Clarissa watches them go and then turns to stare out of the window. She isn't aware of the sparkle of the little stream below, or the arrow-flash of the dipper's flight: all her thoughts are inward. She's frustrated by the sisters' departure. She's worked hard at being best friends with them, especially Fliss: Lady Chadwick. She likes to brag about them to her friends – Admiral Sir Hal has a certain ring to it – but somehow Fliss manages to evade a real closeness. Clarissa suspects that they know that Ralph likes to play the field. He's always had an eye for the ladies, but she's never been able to catch him out. There are always good reasons for his absences, his trips away. She's even suspected his sister-in-law, Lizzie, but Ralph has explanations for his visits to her, especially since his brother died and he's one of the executors of his brother's will.

Clarissa sits back in her chair, sips her tea and looks around her. It would be very satisfying to play Ralph at his own game but she's never been good at the lightness of touch required for a flirtation. She tried it once with Hal but he was humiliatingly kind, bantering, smiling, as if he were humouring a child in a game, and she felt embarrassed and frustrated. As she sits, contemplating the sweetness of revenge, an odd thing happens. A man has come into the coffee shop with a woman and now they sit opposite each other, the woman on the banquette against the wall, and the man facing her. The man is Gus, Susanna's husband.

They immediately embark on an animated conversation while Clarissa watches them, intrigued. It seems so odd that Gus should arrive so quickly after Susanna's departure, and that he should be so taken up with this woman, who looks rather younger and is very pretty. She is talking now, gesticulating, and Gus watches her, nodding encouragingly.

Clarissa feels elated. She remembers how the sisters hurried away from her, how they have resisted any real closeness, and now she sees an opportunity for a different kind of revenge. Not to do with Ralph but simply to pay off a few scores with the Chadwicks.

She pushes back her chair, stands up and, picking up her bag, goes down the few steps so that she is directly behind Gus's chair.

'Hi, Gus,' she says, touching him lightly on the shoulder.

He turns quickly, his expression changing

almost comically to dismay at the sight of her, and she hurries away before he can speak. At the door she glances back and is delighted to see him still looking after her with the anxious expression still on his face.

CHAPTER FOUR

Ed drives beneath the archway of the gatehouse, stops the car, and sits for a moment in the courtyard, staring up at the three-storey, castellated tower. There have been Chadwicks at The Keep for nearly two hundred years. An ancestor, returning from the Far East with a considerable fortune, purchased the ruined hill fort between the moors and the sea, and rebuilt it with the stones lying about the site. The wings, two storeys high and set back on each side of the house, were later additions, along with the courtyard with its high stone walls and gatehouse. Old-fashioned roses and wisteria climb the courtyard walls and the newer wings, but the austere grey tower itself remains unadorned.

Ed sits looking around and smiles a little. Nothing has changed. He feels rather like the prodigal son returning home with very little to show for his absence.

Even as he thinks it, his father and Freddie appear around the side of the house with a golden Labrador at their heels. They are laughing and talking together, and his sense of inadequacy is suddenly sharp. They see him and come towards him and he climbs quickly out of the car, feeling at less of a disadvantage if he's standing. His father shakes his hand, Freddie smiles at him, and Ed bends to stroke the dog, grateful for the distraction. As they stand, talking about his journey, exchanging greetings, Fliss comes out and calls a welcome to him. He goes to greet her and she holds out her arms to him, hugging him, and he's oddly touched and grateful for this sign of affection.

'It's good to see you, Ed,' she says. 'Come on in. We'll sort out your luggage later.'

He follows her into the garden room, where his father and Freddie kick off their boots and give the dog a quick rub down with a rather muddy towel.

'Coffee,' Fliss is saying, going through to the kitchen. 'Would you like some, Ed? Or are you a tea man?'

He doesn't want to feel like a stranger, a guest, so he sits down at the long refectory table without waiting to be asked, smiling at them all, reminding himself that Freddie also has no job and no home at the moment, which brings a small measure of comfort to Ed in his vulnerable state.

'Definitely coffee,' he says. 'Thanks, Fliss.'

He looks around him at the patchwork curtains and matching cushions, the bright rugs on the old flagstones, the dog basket beside the Aga. It's a familiar and comforting scene. But before he can speak, voices are heard in the passage, the door is flung open and a small boy rushes in. He stops suddenly, staring around until he sees Ed sitting at the table.

'Are you Ed?' he demands. 'Is that your car outside?'

'Yes, it is,' says Ed, smiling. 'Do you have a problem with that?'

'No! It's awesome,' he replies solemnly, and everyone laughs. 'Can we go for a ride in it?'

'Well,' begins Ed cautiously, wondering how it might be managed in his two-seater. 'We'll have to see about that.'

'Mummy says you've come all the way from America. Have you brought me a present?'

There's a general protest from all the adults, and Lulu, arriving in time to hear it, is clearly embarrassed.

'Ollie,' she cries, 'that's very rude. Sorry, Ed,' she adds. 'Hi. It's great to see you again. It's been much too long. This is Ollie.'

'It's great to see you, too,' he says, feeling suddenly at ease. 'And no, I haven't brought a present for you, Ollie, because I wasn't sure what you might like so I thought we might go shopping together and you could choose. What d'you think?'

'Awesome!' cries Ollie again.

Ed sees his father's nod of approval, Freddie's amused but slightly quizzical glance, Lulu's smile of pleasure, and he relaxes in his chair and smiles his thanks to Fliss as she pours his coffee.

Round one to the prodigal son, he thinks.

*

Ed's return home is going well. Freddie takes his coffee and retires to the window seat to watch his family. Ollie is unwittingly helping the reunion along. His questions, his eagerness to show this new friend his toys, cover the awkwardness that might have accompanied Ed's explanations and reasons for his return. As it is, Hal and Fliss smile at Ollie's excitement whilst Lulu tries to contain his exuberance. Because it's a Saturday there is plenty of the day left for Ollie to get to know Ed, and presently he agrees to go upstairs to see Ollie's train set whilst Fliss and Hal sort out lunch.

As Ed pushes back his chair he glances across at Freddie, and raises his eyebrows as if wondering if he's going to accompany them, but Freddie gives a little shake of the head. The very slight shrugging of Ed's shoulders makes Freddie feel as if he's being a bit of a spoilsport but he remains where he is, watching them go,

Ollie chattering at the top of his voice. Then Fliss pushes back her chair and Hal watches her, an odd expression on his face. Freddie suspects that they might want to talk about Ed and decides to give them some privacy. He stands up, rinses his mug out and smiles at them.

'Got a few things to do,' he says. 'See you later. Unless I can do anything to help . . .?'

'No, it's all simple stuff,' says Fliss. 'Give us about half an hour.'

Freddie nods and heads back outside, crossing the courtyard and going into the gatehouse. It's been renovated since Fox, the gardener and handyman, lived here back in the fifties, and Freddie goes into a big room that is now both study and sitting room, with a wood-burner in the stone fireplace and bookshelves lining one whole wall. When he moved in, Fliss brought over a box of books that belonged to his great-uncle Theo, also a priest and naval chaplain, and Freddie enjoys looking through them, hoping for inspiration in his own situation.

Now Freddie stands for a moment, hands in his pockets, head bent. He is rather surprised by his feelings: a slight sense of resentment that Ollie should so quickly take to Ed, that Lulu welcomed him with so much affection. He knows that he is being childish and he mutters an imprecation under his breath. His state of mind worries him: his indecision, his disaffection with his ministry. He has no sense of direction.

He sits at the round oak table and thinks, as he so often does in these moments, of his old friend and mentor, Sister Emily, at the Retreat House, Chi-Meur, in north Cornwall. During the worst of the Covid pandemic, Chi-Meur was closed, but now it's opened its doors again and Freddie wonders if he should have a sabbatical there, a few weeks to help him to focus.

He thinks again about Ed, who is able to irritate him so easily, and he wonders why it should be so. Surely his vocation should enable him to take this sort of thing in his stride but, since they were children, Ed's always been able to get under his skin. Freddie feels guilty that he's pleased that Ed is also without a home or a job or a partner, and is angry with himself for being so mean-spirited. He stands up, ducking to avoid the great central beam, and goes to the bookshelf. Not really studying the titles, he takes down a book and looks at it. *The Impact of God: Soundings from St John of the Cross* – one of Theo's books. He opens it at random and sees the translation of the prayer of a Soul in Love.

> Who can free himself from his meanness and
> limitations,
> if you do not lift himself to yourself, my God,
> in purity of love?

How will a person
brought to birth and nurtured in a world of
small horizons,
rise up to you, Lord,
if *you* do not raise him by the hand which
made him?
You will not take from me, my God,
what you once gave me
in your only son, Jesus Christ,
in whom you gave me all I desire;
so I shall rejoice:
you will not delay, if I do not fail to hope.

Freddie takes the book and sits down again at the table: 'meanness and limitations' seem particularly apt just at the moment. He begins to read.

When Fliss knocks at the door, he leaps up, cracks his head on the beam and lets out a howl of frustration.

'Are you OK?' she asks, putting her head round the door.

'Yes,' he answers quickly. 'Yes, of course. Sorry, I got absorbed in something. Is it lunchtime?'

They go out together and she links her arm in his as they cross the courtyard. Her affection soothes but also slightly irritates him because he suspects that there is an element of pity in it. He wants to tell her he's fine, that he's a big boy now, that he can cope with Ed, but she forestalls him.

'I'm really glad you're here,' she tells him. 'Hal always finds Ed a bit tricky. He was always so much Maria's boy. But it's much easier with other people around.'

She squeezes his arm and lets it go, and, slightly taken aback, confused but pleased, he follows her into the house.

CHAPTER FIVE

Ed climbs into his car, drives out of the stable yard, around the courtyard and away down the lane. Lulu and Ollie have set off for school, Fliss and Hal are discussing gardening and taking Honey for a walk, and Freddie has not yet appeared from the gatehouse. Ed is feeling the need to be alone, to escape for a while from this whole new experience of family life. He's gratified by the reception he's been given – especially by small Ollie – but slightly taken off balance by it. He's not used to small children or living in a large family unit and he wants some space.

He drives away, not certain where he's going but remembering that Totnes is the nearest town. Lulu drove him in to show him the photographic studio huddling beneath the castle walls, explaining how, since Covid, she's been running it on her own, and then they wandered round the Friday market amongst the colourful stalls, paused to listen to the buskers, and had coffee in a coffee shop in the medieval high street.

'Bit of a change from New York,' he said, smiling at her across the table.

'I can imagine,' she answered. 'But I love it. Alison keeps telling me I should get out, make a change, but . . . I don't know. It's just my place, I guess.'

He watched her for a moment, sensing a defensiveness. 'And Alison is your sister?

That's right, isn't it? Sorry, there's so many of us I get a bit confused.'

She nodded. 'Big sister. Freddie is eldest, Alison next, then me. Littlest, least and last.'

'And what does Alison do?'

'She's a solicitor in Bristol, married to a doctor. She was always the clever one.'

Ed gave a little shrug. 'I think it's rather cool to have your own photographic studio and to have survived through the pandemic and still be up and running. Sounds like fun.'

'It is, actually. Lots of people are doing Airbnb now, especially around here, and they need photos and videos so it's going quite well. And Dad's really pleased that he can retire and I'm carrying it on.'

As Ed drives into Totnes he thinks about that defensiveness, the 'littlest, least and last', and sympathizes. His is a different situation but he feels a little bit like that about his older brother,

Jolyon: television presenter, happily married, two children, beloved at The Keep. Neither he nor Lulu have talked about their personal lives but there is a kind of unspoken empathy between them, a mutual understanding. Ed is well aware of how much Ollie's presence has helped to ease his way back to his family. Ollie is delighted to have a new cousin, back from America with a sports car and a good instinct for the right kinds of books and toys, and Ed knows he's gaining brownie points. And he's actually enjoying this new experience. He's aware of the family's efforts not to talk about Rebecca, to refrain from asking questions, and he's grateful. It's so difficult maintaining the pretence, keeping his secrets. On the other hand, it's easy being the fun cousin who has no responsibility.

He wonders if Freddie's nose has been put slightly out of joint by Ollie's affection but he isn't showing it. Ed still feels the instinct to tease, to poke and prod, but Freddie isn't rising to Ed's baiting. He'd like to question Freddie about what he plans to do next, what he's thinking and feeling about being without a job, but he's afraid that Freddie might ask him the same question. How good it would be to make a clean breast of things. Perhaps it was foolish of him to believe that he could do it.

Ed parks where Lulu showed him, nearly opposite the photographic studio. He buys a ticket, locks the car and heads off into the town.

Leaving Fliss in the garden room, putting on her boots ready for a session in the kitchen garden, Hal walks out through the stable yard towards the hill, climbing the well-worn paths, crisscrossed with sheep tracks. Mist curls through the valley below, revealing ghostly shapes – slowly moving cattle, feathery tree tops – but here, higher up, the sun is shining. The tors of the moor are visible in the distance, sketched along the horizon, rocks piled by a giant's hand above the bracken-covered slopes. Familiar though it is to Hal, this scene always brings delight: the patchwork of small neat fields and villages, the silvery gleam of river water.

Two rooks, disturbed in their feeding by Honey, flap up, croaking raucously as they go, and Hal walks on, thinking about his family. His sense of responsibility encompasses them all: Lulu trying to plan a new life without Mark, which needs to work for her and Ollie; Freddie, who seems to have lost his way since leaving the navy; Ed, who never lets anyone get too close, who insists that he has several irons in the fire, that this is just a breathing space. Hal knows that all three of them are adults who need to sort out their own lives, but he and Fliss can't help but worry about them, to want what is best – whatever that might be – for them. The pandemic has changed so much, destroyed so much, but he and Fliss are determined that the family must pull together now to get them all back on track.

He pauses to look back down the hill. Thank God for The Keep, he thinks, that small stone fortress, protecting them all. The real problem is that he feels helpless, unable to direct or advise, unsure what is best for these three who are no longer children yet seem so vulnerable.

'If we can just go with it,' Fliss said, 'we can make it a happy time. It's lovely to have them here. Really great to have the house busy, used. *Carpe diem*, and all that. I love it that Ollie is in the nursery where we were when we came back from Kenya. OK, so I don't love the reasons why he and Lulu are here, but we can try to turn it round and make it positive. And dear old

Freddie. I can't blame women for not liking the idea of those long separations, but maybe now he can find somewhere to settle. And Ed . . .'

She paused then, not quite knowing what to say about Ed. Her twins, Bess and Jamie, have fulfilled, happy lives, but Hal knows that she's just as concerned about Ed as she is for her niece and nephew, and he's grateful to her. Ed is such a difficult person to get close to; something about him makes it impossible to question him, to find out about his circumstances. He evades any kind of probing about his work, except that he's in IT, and he seems quite calm about finding another job – if not the one he's applied for in London, then some other. Hal hears his phone ping and he takes it out of his pocket. It's a message from Fliss.

Sooz has offered to bring lunch over. Gus is supplying the wine. Are you happy with that? x

Hal smiles. This is their way of sharing and he is touched by it. He taps out an answer.

Definitely. x

He whistles to Honey and they start the descent. Hal feels calm again: ready to face the day. And what a day it is: late autumn sunshine, a glint of gold on the trees, the flick and flitter of a flock of finches in the furze. It's been strange to see the sky free of aeroplanes: no chalky trails sketched across the blue board of the sky, only a buzzard hovering high above him. Fliss is right: *Carpe diem.*

In the kitchen garden, Fliss pauses from her task of digging in compost. The soil is still warm from the summer and she's planning ahead for next year. She loves it here. Presently she will pick the last of the red and yellow Sunset apples from the cordon trees that grow on the high walls, and there is some kale, too, looking like quill pens, which she will harvest.

As she plans for next spring she's thinking about Ed and Lulu and Freddie: wondering what will happen, how their lives will unfold. The Covid restrictions have eased, much more is open to them now, but there are still difficulties. Lulu talks of getting a flat in Totnes, but there is very little rental accommodation available and it seems foolish to go to the trouble and expense of finding somewhere whilst there is so much room here. But Fliss can see that Lulu might like to have more privacy, the opportunity to meet someone new. It's good to see her getting along so well with Ed, though occasionally Fliss wonders if Freddie is feeling slightly sidelined. Ollie clearly loves his new cousin. It's Ed who is now chosen to read the bedtime story, to go on the school run. Freddie seems perfectly fine with it, but Fliss knows that her nephew doesn't show his feelings readily. Certainly Ed has introduced a new, lighter spirit into their little circle although he and Freddie still maintain the wariness that has always coloured their relationship. It's clear that Ed's sharp witticisms about the Church still irritate Freddie, who finds it difficult to laugh them off. Sometimes she leaps to his defence, which doesn't really help: it embarrasses Freddie and amuses Ed.

Why do relationships have to be so complicated, wonders Fliss, as she puts the fork in the wheelbarrow and pushes it back to the greenhouse. She worries about Lulu, too. Fliss sees that Mark has damaged Lulu's confidence, lowered her self-esteem, and she wonders how it can be restored. Ed's easy-going, cheerful approach to life seems to appeal to Lulu, but Fliss knows that Ed also has his problems. He's evasive about what his future plans are, what jobs he's applying for – the job he was after in London seems not to have come to anything – and what his financial situation is. He's simply staying for just a few weeks, so he doesn't contribute as Freddie and Lulu do, but he's very generous, buying delicious treats, bottles of wine, presents for Ollie.

As she puts the fork away, leans the wheelbarrow against the wall, Fliss is slightly relieved that Ed has messaged to say that he won't be back for lunch. He's decided to explore Totnes and have a walk along the river. She wonders if he plans to meet up with Lulu, who is working at the studio. Freddie has gone to Exeter to meet an old friend so it will be just the four of them, which will be good. Susanna and Gus know the situation and are very tactful. Nevertheless, conversation can sometimes be tricky when it comes to discussing any plans for the future with their young, and Fliss is looking forward to a relaxed lunch.

Whilst she packs two baskets with pâté, cheese, sourdough bread and home-made soup, Susanna is thinking about Gus. He's been just a tad odd recently: preoccupied, jumpy. If it were anyone but Gus she might be a bit suspicious – especially since Clarissa told her that she saw him in Bayards Kitchen with a woman. She dropped it casually into the conversation but there was a kind of awful glee about her manner, a watchfulness in her small brown eyes, that made Susanna feel quite cross.

'Might be anyone,' she answered Clarissa indifferently. 'One of the choir members. Or a client. He's mostly retired, but he still helps Lulu out now and again.'

Clarissa shrugged, made some laughing

remark, but the little seed had lodged and grown. It's unlike Gus to be edgy and she can't think of any good reason for it. At one point she even repeated Clarissa's conversation and watched for his response. Was that a flicker of anxiety in his eyes? But he laughed it off.

'What a poisonous cow that woman is,' he said lightly. 'Poor old Ralph. How does he bear it now that he's retired?'

Susanna found that it was impossible to question him further – it seemed to demean their relationship – but it was clear that there was something on his mind. Now he appears in the kitchen carrying a bottle of wine in each hand, holding them out so that she can see the label.

'Sharpham's Dart Valley Reserve,' he says. 'I thought the occasion demanded something special.'

He looks happy, at ease, and she relaxes.

'It'll be good to see them on their own,' she says. 'There are so many pitfalls at the moment. I wish Freddie could find a parish. I worry about him.'

Gus puts the wine into the baskets and folds his arms around her.

'I know you do,' he says. 'But something will turn up. He needs to want to do the job or he won't be happy.'

She holds him tightly. 'I know that really. But he's such a funny old thing. I feel I can't reach him at the moment.'

He kisses the top of her head, gives her another hug. 'I feel the same, but it will come right. I know it.'

She smiles at him. This is the old Gus, her rock. How foolish to be even momentarily alarmed by Clarissa's poison.

'Sorry,' she says. 'Just having a wobble. OK. Let's get this show on the road.'

CHAPTER SIX

There's a letter waiting for Freddie when he comes into the kitchen the following morning.

'A real letter,' says Ed, making big eyes. 'Actual handwriting on the envelope and everything.'

Freddie takes the letter from Fliss, pretending to ignore Ed whilst overcoming a desire to smack him. He looks at the handwriting and then puts the letter in the back pocket of his jeans. He wonders why he finds Ed's teasing so difficult to cope with and wishes he could be lighter spirited, ready to joke and laugh.

'Hal's taken Honey up on the hill,' Fliss says, clearly aware of the tension. 'Lulu's taken Ollie to school and is going on to the studio. I'm going into Totnes. Very welcome to come with me.'

She glances from one to the other and Freddie suddenly decides that he'd like to do that. To escape from his anxieties and have some company. He'll read his letter later.

'That would be great,' he says. 'Thanks.'

He can see that Ed is hesitating – maybe it's one of those 'Two's company, three is none' moments – then he shakes his head.

'I'll give it a miss,' he says, and Freddie feels a sense of relief.

'I'll grab a jacket,' he says to Fliss, 'and see you out there.'

He glances at Ed as he goes out but Ed is

staring at a message that's just come in on his phone and doesn't notice.

'Do you need to do any shopping?' asks Fliss, as she locks the car. 'I'm going to Halls and the farm shop but we can meet in the Terrace afterwards for coffee.'

'No, I'm fine,' he answers. 'I might get a newspaper. See you later.'

He likes the Terrace Coffee Shop, built on the ruins of the old priory, set above the passageway leading to the high street, with its whitewashed walls and the big stone fireplace. The owners, Rob and Andy, always give them a warm welcome and it's a peaceful place to sit by the windows in the sunshine with the cyclamen in the window boxes. Rob brings him a cappuccino and Freddie takes the letter from his back pocket and settles down to read it. He'd recognized the writing, of course, when

Ed joked about it, but had no intention of telling him that it was from Sister Emily at Chi-Meur, knowing that it would probably raise more amusement, more humorous comments. Now in her eighties, Sister Emily prefers the art of letter writing to emails, and Freddie is glad. It's good to have her letters, to be able to carry them about and reread them. She is his mentor. She keeps him in touch with the news of the retreat house. They now have conferences and weddings, as well as retreats, and his old friend Janna is still looking after the few remaining sisters. Sister Emily knows of his dilemma, that he is in the desert, and her love and support are very special to him. The letter opens with the usual greeting:

Freddie beloved,

I have been holding you in prayer each day at Morning Prayer and again in the silence

> before Compline. Try not to feel too despairing about your resentment towards your cousin when he teases you. Even Christ lost his temper in the temple.
>
> And Ed's teasing is probably masking some inadequacy of his own. Perhaps you could help him. You ask for something to read and I wonder if you might find Michael Mayne's 'Learning to Dance' as uplifting as I do. There's a chapter for each month of the year and I'm finding October particularly life-affirming. This month is the 'Dance of Love'. There's a quote from St John of the Cross. 'When the evening of this life comes, we shall be judged on love.' Very thought-provoking.

St John of the Cross. Ed pauses, folding the letter, remembering what he had been reading earlier. 'Who can free himself from his meanness and limitations . . .' But how could he possibly help Ed, even if he wanted to, which just at the moment he doesn't?

The café door opens and there is Fliss. Rob and Andy are welcoming her, making her coffee, and Freddie gives an inward sigh of relief; glad to be distracted.

'I've cheated,' says Fliss, sitting down, 'and bought pasties for lunch. Hal loves Halls' pasties.'

'Sounds good to me,' answers Freddie. 'So what are we going to do about his birthday? Have you got a plan . . .?'

When they get home Hal is nowhere to be seen but Ed is sitting at the kitchen table, drinking coffee with Honey in attendance. He has an odd expression, preoccupied, wary.

'Hi,' he says. 'So was it fun?'

His tone manages to imply that fun is an unlikely possibility with your aunt in a small market town, but that Freddie might be desperate enough to find it so.

'It depends how you define fun,' answers Freddie equably, helping Fliss unpack the bags. 'I enjoyed it.'

The old antagonism is back and Freddie feels the usual mix of guilt and irritation. He remembers that when they left, Ed was staring at a message on his phone.

'How about you?' he asks. 'Been messaging your friends?'

The look Ed gives him is quick, suspicious, almost guilty, and Freddie is taken aback. He responds to it instinctively, thinking of Sister Emily's letter.

'Fliss has bought pasties for lunch,' he says casually, 'so that's easy. How about we take Honey out on the hill to get our appetites up?'

Ed is still looking at him with that odd expression and now he gives a kind of facial shrug, lifting his eyebrows, pulling down the corners of his mouth.

'Why not?' he says almost with indifference.

'Great,' says Freddie. 'I'll go and change my shoes.'

When he gets into the gatehouse he pauses for a moment, surprised at himself. He takes Sister Emily's letter from his pocket and drops it on the table, then notices that there are a couple more lines on the back of the sheet. He picks it up again and reads her words.

> PS. This book might not be for you, Freddie beloved, and don't worry if it isn't. But who knows? Maybe it's time you learned to dance.

He stares at the words for a moment, then he tucks the letter in between the leaves of a book, changes his shoes, and goes back out to find Ed and Honey.

Fliss watches them go with a mix of surprise and pleasure. It would be such a relief if these two could find an amicable way forward, rather than the bantering and bickering that is never very far away in their relationship. It's odd that she's more worried about Ed than she is about Freddie. Freddie seems to have lost his sense of direction but there's something about Ed, a continual brightness, the need to keep everyone laughing, that she suspects is a veneer to hide something. But what? She and Hal have talked about it but never come to a conclusion. Ed doesn't seem too heartbroken about the break-up with Rebecca, and he doesn't seem to be short of money.

'I'm not even sure what it is he does,' Hal said. 'I find the IT stuff very confusing. He baffles me with science. I'm just worried that he's done something foolish, like when he lost Maria's investments, and he's just keeping his head down.'

'You mean he's hiding from creditors?' Fliss was momentarily alarmed but instinct told her that this is not the reason for Ed's visit.

Hal shook his head. 'I don't really think so, but that's the trouble with Ed. You just never quite know. There's an instability.'

Now, as she puts away the shopping, Fliss thinks about that remark. It's true; all that glitter and gleam, smoke and mirrors, but who is the real Ed? She hates the idea that he can't confide in them but there's little she can do: she's not his mother. At least she can offer him refuge. Maybe Freddie can win his confidence, and she wonders what they're talking about, out there on the hill.

*

Following Hal into Bayards Kitchen, Susanna sees Clarissa too late to beat a retreat. She waves enthusiastically, indicating the spare chairs, and Susanna waves back, cursing under her breath.

'At least she's got Ralph with her,' says Hal, as they order their coffee at the counter. 'Want a croissant?'

'Tempting,' she answers, 'but I shall resist. How about you?'

He shakes his head. 'Fliss said she might get pasties for lunch. Come on. Once more unto the breach and all that.'

'How nice to see you,' cries Clarissa brightly as they sit down. 'But odd to see you together without Gus or Fliss.'

She glances inquisitively between them as if demanding an explanation.

'I know,' Hal smiles blandly at her. 'But there we are. You've found us out at last. We shall just have to beg you to keep it to yourselves.'

Susanna wants to laugh out loud at Clarissa's expression, but manages not to simply because Ralph looks so uncomfortable.

'How are you?' he asks.

'You must be so busy,' Clarissa says before they can answer. 'I was saying to Ralph that it must be so odd having your adult children living with you again. I do admire you. I can't see Selina wanting to come back to live with us.'

There's an awkward little silence whilst the words 'And I can quite imagine why!' hang unspoken in the air.

'Fliss and I are really enjoying it,' answers Hal calmly. 'You rarely get the privilege of having young people around when you get to our ages. We're making the most of it.'

Clarissa is silenced and the coffee arrives, so there's a moment before any of them speak again.

'So how are you doing, Ralph?' asks Susanna,

managing to refrain from using the words 'good works'. 'I saw something about you in the paper raising funds for Totnes Caring. Well done.'

He smiles at her. 'Thank you, but it's not just me. They're a great team.'

'It certainly takes up a lot of his time,' says Clarissa tartly, and there's another awkward silence.

'And how's Gus?' she asks then, with a kind of concerned sympathy, and Susanna's heart sinks, hoping she's not going to comment again on seeing him with a young woman.

'Gus is another busy fellow,' replies Hal before she can speak. 'It's great that he can be singing again. Thank goodness we can all get out and about after lockdown. Let's hope we don't get another spike this winter.'

Covid dominates the conversation for a moment and then Ralph says that they should be moving. Clarissa looks disappointed, but they've finished their coffee and Ralph is already standing up, collecting coats and bags.

'There seemed to be a certain sense of tension around all that,' observes Hal, sipping his coffee. 'Is there something I should know?'

Susanna fiddles with the biscuit in her saucer, notices that the music in the background is '50 Ways to Leave Your Lover' and gives a little snort of exasperation.

'She saw Gus in here with a young woman and now she's hinting that he might be playing around.'

'And is he?' asks Hal, grinning. 'Why can't I imagine Gus playing around?'

'Thanks for that,' she says. 'I did actually mention what Clarissa said but he was almost indifferent. Just said how poisonous she is.'

'And?' Hal is watching her, waiting.

'I expect it was a choir member, but the odd thing was that it was an afternoon when he said he was going to Exeter.'

'So how did he explain that?'

'He didn't. I didn't question him. It was too . . . I don't know . . . well, degrading. Do you know what I mean?'

'Yes, I think so,' says Hal after a moment. 'After all these years it's too ludicrous to think about.'

'Yes,' she says gratefully. 'It would undermine both of us.' She gives a little shiver. 'The trouble is that Clarissa's already sown a nasty seed of suspicion. And I have to admit that Gus is being just a little bit odd.'

'How d'you mean?'

'Well, nothing I could really put my finger on, but a bit distracted. Keeping his phone under strict control.' She shrugs. 'I'm probably being paranoid, but that's what I mean. That poisonous cow has sown a little seed of doubt and I can't quite uproot it.'

Hal is silent for a moment, leaning back, glancing around him.

'Does Fliss know?'

'No,' Susanna answers quickly. 'And I don't really want her to. Sorry, Hal. Not fair to tell you then ask you to keep it to yourself. Gosh, I hate this.'

'OK,' he says calmly. 'That's not a problem. I don't believe it for a moment, but mightn't it be better to be absolutely open with Gus? He'll understand.'

'I know, and I do think about it, but then it's so humiliating to actually ask the question.'

'Yes, I get that. Where is he, by the way?'

'He's at home. I just dashed out to get a birthday card for someone, and there you were buying some wine. I felt we deserved coffee.'

'We did.' He smiles at her. 'How about both

of you coming over for supper? Ed's making one of his famous Thai green curries.'

'That sounds good,' she answers. For some silly reason she feels a bit weepy. She hates feeling like this about Gus and it would be good to have a real family evening. 'Yes,' she says. 'It's a date.'

CHAPTER SEVEN

November

It's Hal who lights the first fire of the year in the hall. He's already built a wigwam of kindling on the granite hearthstone, tucking a firelighter deep within it, and carefully placing twigs and small logs on the flames as they take hold. There's a large log basket in its own alcove within the deep recess of the fireplace and it's his job to make certain that it's kept piled high with dry logs throughout the winter.

Two high-backed sofas, heaped with cushions, face each other across the long, low oak table and at the end of it a deep comfortable armchair stands opposite the fireplace. It's a room within a room, a warm cosy space within the vaster, draughty spaces of the hall. Hal sits on the little stool beside the alcove, watching the flames take hold, as they creep along the small twigs, licking around the smaller logs.

He wishes that Susanna had never told him about her suspicions regarding Gus. Keeping it from Fliss has been much more difficult than he anticipated and once or twice she's asked if he has something on his mind. Luckily there's always Ed to fall back on, anxieties about his future and so on, but nevertheless he's not happy with the deception. His birthday supper went well, everyone cheerful, and Gus certainly didn't look like a man with a guilty secret. In fact, it's Ed who is behaving more like that:

giving a little start if his phone buzzes, looking preoccupied, and not quite so ready to tease Freddie. And Freddie seems to have no direction, no focus.

Hal sighs and leans forward to place another log on the fire, which is now blazing up in a very satisfactory way. It's been a warm November, glorious autumn colours, bronze and yellow and red, but now Storm Arwen has swept in and most of the trees stand bare and exposed. Fliss and Freddie are sweeping up leaves, a job they both enjoy, and Honey is with them, Lulu is fetching Ollie from school and they will all be coming in to tea. Hal places a few more logs on the fire, wonders where Ed is, and goes into the kitchen to fill the kettle.

Ed is standing at his bedroom window, staring across the meadow to the line of trees at the hedge's boundary. Ollie's bedroom is directly above his, in the nursery, and Ed looks at the trees, trying to make out the faces and shapes that Ollie sees. It's a still, quiet afternoon and as he stares intently he can begin to see, although now that the leaves are nearly gone it's not so easy to make out the faces amongst the branches. There's a big twiggy profile – jutting nose, big chin – and he sees an ivy-covered tree that looks as if it is dancing, arms flung up high.

His phone rings. Ed stares at the caller's number but makes no attempt to answer it. After it's stopped ringing a message pings in.

> Come on, Ed. Please answer. I can see you're ghosting me so stop this and get in touch. Nick's told me you are back but no one seems to know where you are. I know there are all sorts of problems but can't we just work it out? I've missed you. I know you've got family in the West Country so maybe I can track you down. Love you. x

Ed turns away from the window, filled with panic. 'Panic and emptiness' – E. M. Forster's words seem to sum up Ed's life just now and he feels a ridiculous desire to burst into tears. He needs courage, strength, but from where shall he find them? His life has been such a mess. He stares at the message and wonders if it is possible to wipe the slate clean and start again. Is it possible? Where could he start? The mere idea makes him shiver. He hears voices, Ollie calling out his name, and, putting his phone in his pocket, Ed goes down to meet him.

As soon as Freddie comes into the kitchen from the garden room he can see that all is not well with Lulu. Hal has already begun to organize the tea tray and though he is talking to Lulu, Freddie can see that she's not really concentrating. There's a little frown between her brows and she's clearly distracted. Hal is taking the tray, calling some instruction about making the tea over his shoulder, but she doesn't seem to be listening.

'Everything OK?' Freddie asks lightly. 'I'll make some tea, shall I?'

She looks at him, glances quickly around. 'I've had an email from Mark,' she says. 'He wants to come and see Ollie. He's even asking if he can stay. I mean, seriously? We hardly ever hear from him, it's been two years, but suddenly it's like nothing ever happened.'

'Have you answered the email?'

'No, of course not. I was just leaving the studio when it came in. It's just knocked me off balance.'

'Well, that's reasonable,' Freddie says calmly. 'Don't panic about this. We'll sort something out. You're in control here.'

'It's not that I don't want him to see Ollie, it's just that he's been so casual about it.'

Freddie tries to think how she can deal with this, but before he can speak Fliss comes in, pulling a jersey on.

'It's very chilly,' she says. 'I'm glad Hal has lit the fire. Are you coming?'

'Yes, of course,' answers Freddie. 'We're making tea. Well, coffee for Ed, of course.'

'I'll see what Hal's taken through,' she says, and goes out.

'Let's talk about this later,' Freddie says. 'I imagine you won't be telling Hal and Fliss just yet?'

'God no!' says Lulu. 'I need time to process it. But I simply can't have him here. I mean, he just walked out. Told me he'd been having this affair with Anneke for months and that he was going back to the Netherlands with her. Good-bye and thanks for all the fish.'

She looks angry, hurt, and turns quickly away as Ollie comes running in.

'Granny's got some good games,' he shouts. 'Come and see, Mummy.'

'I'm coming,' she answers. 'I'll be right there. Just finding that cake you like. Go and tell Granny I'm just coming.'

He disappears again and Freddie puts his arm round Lulu's shoulder and gives her a quick hug.

'Let's talk later when Ollie's in bed. But try not to panic. We're all here.'

She gives a huge sigh and he feels her relax.

'Sorry,' she says. 'I'm being a bit crazy. You're right. What can he do?'

'Good,' he says. 'Don't worry. We'll set Ed on him. That'll show him.'

She gives a little smile. 'Thanks, Freddie. I'm OK now. Can you make Ed's coffee and I'll do the tea?'

When they come into the hall Ollie is sitting on a stool at the end of the long, low table, with Ed and Fliss sitting on each side on the sofas and they are playing a very noisy game of snap. They barely glance up, and Lulu is pleased to sit at the other end of the sofa beside the fire with Honey, watching Hal dealing with the plates and mugs.

She hadn't expected to be so affected by Mark's email. All the pain and resentment has come flooding back, along with a fear that this life that she has made with Ollie and her family might be disrupted. Of course, it would be good if Mark and Ollie could establish a closer relationship, but Ollie was only three when Mark left and, with Covid restrictions, visiting has been non-existent. It's been clear that Mark has very little interest in his child and Lulu wonders what has changed now and feels another pang of anxiety. But watching the scene around the table, she feels calmer. She drops her shoulders, takes a deep breath. How lucky she is to have such a supportive family.

Hal leans forward. 'He's picked it up very quickly,' he says, indicating the triumphant Ollie. 'He's already learning how to cheat.'

They both laugh and Lulu sips her tea. Of course she will tell them all about Mark getting in touch, but not before she's had a proper talk alone with Freddie. That will be difficult this evening but perhaps tomorrow they can slip away, make a plan. She takes another deep breath and settles into the corner of the sofa.

Fliss looks around at them all and thinks how delighted her grandmother, Freddy Chadwick, would be to see them all here, another generation finding sanctuary at The Keep. Though they are all uncertain how their lives will go forward yet, for this time, they are safe. Fliss feels so lucky to have them here. Her own children are far away. Jamie works at the Foreign Office and is in Dubai, and Bess and her husband and children are in Paris, but she's hoping that they might be home for Christmas if restrictions allow. She misses them all so much, and facetiming is better than nothing, but how she longs to see them, to hug them.

'Granny, it's your turn.' Ollie is tugging at her arm and she smiles down at him and picks up her cards.

CHAPTER EIGHT

Ed is walking in the gardens at Dartington Hall. Freddie and Lulu brought him here to have coffee at the Green Table café, reminding him of old times when he used to visit before he went to the States. He likes it here, and often comes on fine days to buy a takeaway coffee and sit in the sunshine. Now, as he walks, his mind is locked on to the secret he carries with him, his longing to be free from it and his cowardice, which makes freedom almost impossible.

He is barely aware of the beauty around him: the courtyard and medieval hall, the gardens in their late autumn glory revealing breathtaking views across the distant countryside. He's thinking of that latest text.

I shall find you, Ed. You can run but you can't hide. x

And even as he rounds the path that leads to the statue of Flora, he sees him. Tall, short dark hair, he is putting an offering of a large bronze-coloured leaf on the pedestal at Flora's feet. He turns before Ed can move and he smiles, holds out a hand as one might to a frightened animal.

'Don't look so surprised,' he says. 'You told me about your family in happier days so it wasn't too hard to find you. Chadwick is quite a big name round here. I must admit, though, that this is a lucky strike. I'm staying at the Hall. Very comfortable. The food's good.'

Automatically, Ed stretches out his hand and it's taken and held firmly.

'Xander,' he says. 'It's just . . . I didn't know how . . .'

Then he is being held and he feels weak with relief, with happiness.

'You always were a fool,' says Xander, releasing him. 'People are coming. Let's walk.'

They climb the steps and walk quickly across the grass to the temple that stands beneath the trees, looking out across the hills. They sit together on the wooden bench and Xander looks at him again and begins to laugh.

'Only you, Ed,' he says. 'Why didn't you let me know you were home?'

Ed shakes his head, staring down the grassy slope, hands clasped between his knees.

'Too ashamed,' he says. 'I was such a bloody fool. I bankrupted my mother with my ill-judged investments, let everybody down and ran away.'

Xander sighs. 'How long have we been friends? What age were we when we were choristers at Salisbury? Come on, Ed. This is me. I'm not going to let you hide any longer. You know that, don't you?'

Ed nods slowly. 'I do know it and I don't want to hide. But you said it yourself. Chadwick is a big name around here and it's going to be very hard to announce to my father and Fliss, not to mention the rest of my cousins, that I'm gay.'

He tries to imagine the scene, his father's reaction, Freddie's face, and all his old fear returns.

Xander touches his arm. 'I get it, Ed. I really do. But you can't keep running, and this is the twenty-first century. It's not a big deal any more. At least, it shouldn't be. And I'm here waiting for you.'

Ed tries to imagine the wonderful feeling of telling the truth, of being free of this dead weight, of taking Xander to meet his family, but it's almost too much: it's been so long.

'Come on,' says Xander. 'Let's go and grab a takeaway coffee from the Green Table and stroll around a bit.'

He leans across, kisses Ed lightly on the cheek, then they get up and walk away together.

Lulu and Freddie are driving up on to the moor. Out past Buckfast Abbey, through Hembury Woods, and up on to Holne Moor. In the back of Freddie's car, Honey sits up, looking expectantly through the window. She knows this road.

'I'm quite glad that Ed didn't want to come,' says Lulu. 'I just wanted this to be you and me so that we could talk about Mark.'

'So did I,' answers Freddie, as they bump over the cattle grid on to the moor. 'The person in the back can't hear properly and the front-seat passenger has to keep translating. Anyway, I think he's got something on his mind and needs some headspace.'

Lulu stares out at the spaces of gold and brown and rust: in the sunlight the dead bracken seems to be on fire and the distant tors are only just defined, blue-grey shapes against the brighter blue of the clear sky. There are sheep like white boulders grazing, and a group of ponies prance and kick up their heels, then stand still to watch the car pass by. Freddie drives slowly so that he too might enjoy the scene, then backs into the little space that was once part of a quarry and switches off the engine. The leat runs here, and hawthorn trees, bowed and shaped by the westerly winds, stand just above the quarry.

'This is Mum's favourite place,' Lulu says. 'She and Dad got engaged up here somewhere.'

'I think I remember her telling me that,' says Freddie. 'Good spot for it. Let's give Honey a walk before she breaks the window.'

'It's great that the choir is rehearsing again,' he says, as they free Honey and she races ahead beside the leat. 'They've got a Christmas production coming up at Dartington and Dad's just full of it.'

'Oh,' says Lulu, 'so that explains his high spirits. He seems to be particularly jolly just recently.'

'He's missed singing,' says Freddie. 'So come on. What's bugging you about Mark's email? It's not as if you're not in touch. Not that often, I know, but it's not quite out of the blue, is it?'

Lulu hunches herself into her jacket. It's not cold but there's a cool breeze.

'No,' she answers slowly, 'but there's something a bit different about this one. He says he's looking forward to seeing us. That it's been too long, and he's asking if he can stay, which is just not on. I simply couldn't cope with it. The trouble is that him being in the Netherlands, plus Covid, has made it very easy for him not to visit. It hasn't seemed to bother him at all till now, but suddenly there's this keenness. Ollie was only three when he left and he barely remembers him.'

'Are you really saying that you think Mark is regretting his decision and wants to come back?'

'Yes. No. Oh, I don't know.' Lulu sounds stressed. 'It's just a bit weird, that's all. And you know Mark. He's just so strong-willed. He always does it his way.'

'Well, that's in the past,' says Freddie firmly. 'You're no longer together, he can't insist he stays at The Keep, and although he must have reasonable access to Ollie there's absolutely no way he can force his way back into your life.'

'What if he should want to take Ollie to the Netherlands?' she asks, her voice full of fear.

Freddie snorts derisively. 'The courts would definitely have something to say about that. And so, I imagine, would Anneke. If he's regretting his decision that's his problem, not yours. What's he actually saying?'

'Stuff about missing us, and catching up with Ollie, especially with Christmas coming up. Just stuff, really. But he wants to make a plan and if I try to put him off he might just turn up anyway.'

'That would be a very stupid thing to do. Don't let him bully you, Lu.'

'But I can't refuse to let him see Ollie.'

'No, but we'll all be around when he does. You don't have to be frightened of him.'

'It's not so much frightened, it's that old thing of him making me feel inadequate.'

'It's called bullying,' says Freddie. 'You're not inadequate. You're running a successful business and raising a happy, well-balanced child. We'll plan a reply and take it from there.' He puts his arm around her shoulders and gives her a quick hug. 'Come on, let's catch Honey up.'

Lulu nods. She takes a calming breath, and follows him along the leat.

Clarissa is in Bayards Kitchen, the Cider Press coffee shop, seated on one of the long benches, when Susanna and Fliss come in. She sees them at once, waves delightedly, so that they are unable to turn and make a quick exit.

They order coffee and then join her, trying to appear as pleased to see her as she is to see them.

'This is really nice,' she says, as they sit down and take off their masks. 'I haven't seen you for ages. How are you both?'

'Fine,' answers Fliss. 'We're all absolutely fine. How about you and Ralph?'

'Well, he's busy as usual.' Clarissa makes a disgruntled face. 'I was hoping he might come with me this morning but someone phoned about some charity event and off he went.'

'All those good works,' says Fliss, sighing sympathetically.

'Well, it keeps him busy, I suppose.' She glances at Susanna. 'How's Gus? I saw him in Totnes the other day, in one of the art galleries. I nearly went in to say hi, but he was having such a good time with one of the assistants, I decided not to intrude.'

To Fliss's surprise, Susanna makes no retort, but she looks almost upset, and it's Fliss who says: 'He's really enjoying being able to sing again. Lots of the choir members work in the town. Gus knows everyone.'

'Yes,' agrees Susanna, who seems to have

pulled herself together. 'That's true. They've got a big event coming up in the Hall and they're all so excited about it. It's so good to have all these things happening after lockdown.'

Clarissa seems chagrined by this response and they talk about other things, whilst from time to time she hints that a Christmas get-together would be such fun. At last, to their relief, she gets up to go.

Fliss looks at her sister. 'So what's all that about?' she asks. 'You looked a bit odd when she was talking about Gus.'

Susanna sits for a moment staring down at her coffee.

'She'd already told me a few weeks ago that she saw Gus here with a pretty young woman. Then the next time I saw her I was here, having bumped into Hal, so we came in for some coffee. Clarissa was with Ralph. She asked about

Gus again, made a bit of a thing about it, all false concern and sympathy.'

Fliss looks puzzled. 'Hal didn't tell me that. I wonder why not.'

'Because I asked him not to,' says Susanna. 'It was silly and embarrassing, and I haven't been able to bring myself to ask Gus outright because it sounds . . .' – she shrugs – 'I don't know, kind of suspicious and weird, especially when I first told him what Clarissa said, and he just laughed and batted it away as an example of her being poisonous. But he's been so odd lately. A bit hyper, as if he's keeping a secret, and I don't quite know how to handle it. And now this. You're right, Gus knows loads of people, and he's always jokey, but this seems a bit different. Sorry. I shouldn't have asked Hal to keep it secret. That was wrong of me. It's just that I feel a fool.'

'It's OK,' says Fliss, but she feels a sense of

relief. There has been a caginess about Hal lately that she couldn't quite understand. 'I'm glad that you told me, though. Keeping secrets can be dangerous. Why don't you simply tell him what Clarissa has been hinting at and ask him straight out? I bet he'll roar with laughter and it's absolutely nothing. This isn't like you, Sooz. Or Gus. Don't let this stuff poison your relationship. It can if you're not careful.'

Susanna nods. She looks a bit tearful. 'I know you're right. I have wanted to, but it's just that I never quite know how to begin.'

'Just ask him, but make it a bit jokey. He knows what Clarissa's like.'

'I will.' Susanna seems to make up her mind. She sits up straighter and finishes her coffee.

'Good,' says Fliss. 'So where is Gus at the moment?'

'Sweeping up leaves,' answers Susanna. 'Well, he was when I left home.'

'OK, then,' says Fliss. 'Here's the plan. We go and buy some delicious bits in the deli and you and Gus come over for some lunch.'

'Sounds good to me,' her sister replies. 'But don't expect me to have asked him by then. I shall need to choose my moment.'

'Fine,' says Fliss, and they put on their masks and go out together.

CHAPTER NINE

Freddie beloved,

So here we are, almost the end of November and in Michael Mayne's book the month of November is the Dance of Faith. And how much we need faith. We are all pilgrims, but if we can keep trusting we are vouchsafed people for the journey. I've often found, when I look back, that when I think that I've been helping someone in fact it is he or she who has been strengthening me. Which is why dancing is so important: it's such a joyous thing, and 'how can we know the dancer from the dance?'

Since Chi-Meur opened to do weddings and even corporate events we are very busy. The setting here is so beautiful and all our guests love it. I have to admit that I rather enjoy it too. I like the bustle, though poor Clem is looking a little bit frazzled lately. Tilly remains her calm, cheerful self, although those two little ones are a handful and Jakey's having the usual teenager moments! So nice that we have young people living here.

Everyone sends their love to you.

It's time for Evening Prayer and I must go.

You are surrounded with love and prayers,

Sr Emily xx

Freddie sits beside the fire reading Sister Emily's letter, deep in thought, when he hears the knock at the door. He glances at his watch:

nearly nine o'clock, rather late for visitors. He gets up and opens the door. Ed is standing outside. He looks both anxious and excited, as if he is suppressing some deep emotions. Freddie tries not to look surprised but opens the door wider and steps aside.

'Come in,' he says. 'I thought you were going to the Cott with Fliss and Hal.'

'I changed my mind,' says Ed. 'Lulu and Ollie have gone to one of their sleepovers with Gus and Susanna so I've seized the moment. There's something I want to discuss with you, if you're OK with that.'

'Fine,' says Freddie. 'Glass of wine? I'm having a rather good Shiraz, compliments of Hal.'

'Yes,' says Ed quickly. 'Thank you. That might be good.' He looks around him at the fire, the bookshelves, the big table. 'It's really nice in here, isn't it?'

'I like it,' says Freddie, pouring a second glass. 'Come and sit down.'

They sit either side of the fire and Freddie wonders how to proceed, but Ed forestalls him.

'This is a bit weird,' he says. 'And I'm just going to go with it. The thing is, I'm gay. Nobody in the family knows because I've never been able to bring myself to tell them. After all those awful things happened, I just ran away but I don't think I can go on carrying this any longer.'

Freddie is taken completely off guard. He tries to take it in but is struggling, whilst Ed watches him anxiously.

'So Rebecca?' he asks at last. 'We all thought you were in a relationship with her.'

Ed shakes his head impatiently. 'She was a front. She's a very good friend and let me use her as a smokescreen. I was in a relationship but I just felt such a shit that I ran away from him too.'

Freddie takes a breath, prays for wisdom. 'But why did you feel that it needed to be a secret? There's no problem here, Ed.'

Ed stares at him. 'Seriously? You mean you're not shocked or . . . anything?'

'Why on earth should I be?' asks Freddie.

Ed pauses, then begins to laugh. 'I can't believe this. I'd worked myself up to all sorts of reaction – shock, disbelief, I don't know what.'

'Then you've misjudged me,' answers Freddie calmly, 'though I can imagine you might have some qualms about telling Hal, but only because you've hidden it so well from everybody.'

Ed takes a long swallow from his glass and Freddie can see that his hand is shaking slightly.

'So why now?' he asks. 'What was the trigger point?'

Ed stares at him and then laughs. 'I can see that I've totally underestimated you. Yes, you're right. The friend I was with before my flight to the States has discovered that I'm home and has been messaging me.'

'And?' Freddie asks after a long pause.

'He knew all about my family here and when I didn't respond he tracked me down. We met up by chance at Dartington. He's staying at the Hall.' Another silence. 'He wants us to be together again, but openly, and I want it too.'

'That's great,' says Freddie. He's very moved by Ed's disclosures, touched that he has been able to confide in him after all the difficulties there have been between them. 'So the next step is to tell the family. You haven't told me his name.'

'It's Alexander. Everyone calls him Xander.'

'Fine. So we need to make a plan. First tell Hal and Fliss and Lulu, then arrange a meeting. Is Xander still at the Hall?'

Ed nods. He looks alarmed. 'We can't all meet here. Not for the first time.'

Now it's Freddie who begins to laugh. 'I agree. Much too intimidating for a first meeting. It needs to be on neutral territory. But first you need to tell them. Do you need moral support for that?'

'Yes,' says Ed quickly. 'No. I don't know. Your reaction has taken me by surprise. I thought . . . well, I don't know what I thought, but I just need to take it in.'

'But don't leave it too long,' says Freddie. 'Don't lose your impetus and let anxiety back in. I'm very happy to meet Xander if you both think it might be helpful.'

'Yes,' says Ed. 'That might be a good idea. I'll talk to him. Thanks, Freddie.'

'Good,' says Freddie, 'but I definitely know what the next step is.' Ed looks puzzled. 'Another glass of wine. Drink up.'

After Ed has gone, Freddie sits staring into the fire, thinking, about Ed and about Sister Emily's letter. This will heal the ongoing rift between him and Ed; it explains Ed's brittleness, the veneer, the wariness. Something has changed and they will all be strengthened by it. Freddie feels a huge sense of peace. Perhaps, after all, he is learning to dance.

Supper is over, Ollie has settled down to sleep at last, and there is time to talk. And Lulu knows what the subject must be.

'Mark wants to come over,' she says abruptly. 'He says he wants to see us and he's asked if he can stay at The Keep. It's totally out of the blue and I don't know what to say.'

Her parents stare at her in surprise. 'When?' asks Gus.

'Before Christmas. And I just don't see how it can work.'

'He can't come to The Keep,' says Susanna, firmly. 'Good heavens, it's two years since he was here. I know Covid has caused problems but he could have come over this summer. And he's hardly ever in touch.'

'It sounds weird, as if things have gone a bit wrong for him, and suddenly he's all friendly,' says Lulu. 'But I can't stop him seeing Ollie.'

'But not necessarily at The Keep. He'll have to stay somewhere locally.'

'You know what he's like,' says Lulu. 'He's always so strong about what he wants to do.'

'He's a bully,' says Gus calmly. 'But you need have no fear. If he wants to come over and stay somewhere nearby, then Ollie can see him, but not alone. Ollie can hardly remember him, so you'd have to be there and one of us would be there with you, too.'

Susanna sits down on the sofa beside her and puts an arm around Lulu.

'I'd almost forgotten how intimidating he can be,' says Lulu, feeling as though she might cry. 'It's crazy but he just doesn't give in until he's got his way.'

'Well, he won't get it this time. Luckily, you're not on your own. He can't simply invite himself to The Keep. Don't panic, Lulu. He can't hurt you now.'

'It was all beginning to work out,' she says. 'I don't think Ollie cares any more, and I was getting over feeling so inadequate. And I've met this lovely guy who's just opened an art gallery in the town. I really thought we were moving on.'

'You are,' says Susanna. 'This is not going to stop you. I know you feel you must keep the channels open between him and Ollie, but there are ways to do that. It would help if Mark sent him a card or a present sometimes. He even forgot his birthday.'

'I know,' says Lulu miserably, 'but even so, I won't stop that kind of contact. I just don't get why he should want to meet up now, out of the blue, after two years.'

'I think you're right: something's gone wrong for him,' says Gus. 'He's fallen out with Anneke – perhaps she didn't like being bullied either – or maybe he's lost his job and this would be an easy route back. He's thinking you're at The Keep, why not him too? Or something like that. Anyway, it's not going to happen.'

'Shall we compose an answer?' suggests Susanna. 'Obviously it needs to be coming from you but we could help make it a bit punchy.'

She and Gus both watch Lulu, concerned and loving, and she smiles at them. 'Yes,' she says. 'Let's try that. Thanks. I feel much better now.'

Susanna gets up to make a cup of tea and Lulu breathes a sigh of relief. She knows it's silly to be so anxious but she simply couldn't bear that Mark's undermining her should begin all over again.

Gus smiles at her. 'We need some music,' he says.

Softly, the Andante from Shostakovich's Piano Concerto No. 2 drifts into the silence, and Lulu rests her head against the cushion and feels a sense of peace.

CHAPTER TEN

December

Ed and Xander are walking in the Dartington Hall gardens on a cold sunny day. The dogwood burns crimson against the greys and browns of the leafless shrubs, and coppery leaves lie thick upon the ground.

'I still can't believe it,' says Xander. 'That you've told them and everything is OK. It's just utterly amazing.'

'It is,' says Ed. He wants to reach out and

grasp Xander's hand but feels that it's rather too public. 'Dad was silent for a moment, like I told you, and then he just got up and held out his arms to me. That's so not like Dad. I mean, we still shake hands when we meet up or when I go away. And he was just so completely understanding. He said, "It must have been so tough for you." I really thought I was going to cry. It was like Freddie. He was just so amazing, so understanding. I thought he'd be a bit, you know, sarky.'

'You've probably never seen the priest in him,' says Xander. 'I'm looking forward to meeting him. I have to say I feel a bit anxious about it now it's a reality, but it will be so good to get it over.'

'The whole question is where,' says Ed. 'I really can't decide where we'd all be most natural. Maybe Freddie is right and it should be on neutral ground. I'm afraid it might be a bit overwhelming otherwise.'

They've reached the Temple and they sit down on the bench, looking down the grassy slope to the field beyond.

'I love this place,' says Xander. 'In a weird way it feels like a homecoming. After all, I am a country boy. Listen, Ed. I've been thinking about the meeting and I've decided that I want to risk The Keep. After all, why not? It's much the easier thing to do than all sitting in a coffee shop or a pub. Shall we?'

Xander turns to look at him, and their hands meet on the bench between them and hold tightly.

'Right,' says Ed, feeling a surge of terror and elation. 'It'll be fine. We can do this.'

'Great,' says Xander, smiling at him. 'It's going to be so good, Ed. Trust me.'

'The crazy thing was,' says Hal to Fliss, 'that once he said it, everything just fell into place.

All that secrecy, withholding himself, was just self-protection.'

They're sitting in the kitchen, which is always kept warm by the Aga, and Honey is asleep in her basket.

'I know,' she answers him. 'I feel the same. Just a huge relief. I'm looking forward to meeting Xander. But I wonder what will happen next. Will they go back to London?'

'I asked Ed that this morning. Xander works in IT at the same company where Ed used to be, and he's working from home. He's suggesting that Ed should go and ask them for a job. Ed thought that if they agreed, he and Xander could stick around here for a bit with perhaps a weekly visit to London to check in. It seems like a lot of people work like that now.'

'That would be great,' says Fliss. 'We could really get to know Ed properly, and Xander too.'

Hal grins at her. 'Are you suggesting that he might come here?'

She laughs. 'We need to meet him first, but I must admit that the thought did just cross my mind, until they get settled.'

'Why not?' says Hal. 'Come one, come all. It's what The Keep does best.'

Susanna watches Gus through their open bedroom door. He's been elated and secretive all day and she can no longer hold back these foolish fears. She pushes the door wide open, and Gus springs round, shuts the wardrobe door behind him and stares at her guiltily.

'Gus,' she says, trying to keep her voice steady. 'I can't cope with all this secrecy and silence stuff any longer. What's it all about? Are you seeing another woman?'

His look of disbelief and amazement would have made her laugh on any other occasion, but not this time. He comes round the end of the bed and holds out his hands to her.

'Darling Sooz,' he says. 'Don't be silly. Whatever's brought this on?'

'Clarissa said she saw you up at Bayards with a young woman, and then again in one of the art galleries in Totnes. And you've been so strange. All secretive and kind of hyper.'

She sits down on the end of the bed, and he sits down beside her and takes her hands, holding them tightly. Unexpectedly she begins to cry and he puts his arms round her, his lips to her hair.

'OK,' he says. 'It was going to be a surprise but I see that I shall have to come clean.'

Letting her go, he gets up, walks round to the wardrobe and takes out a rectangular package.

'It was meant for you for Christmas, but I can't bear to see you like this.'

He tears away the packaging and holds it up.

It's a beautiful watercolour of a hawthorn tree, bent and shaped by winds, bright with scarlet berries, against a moorland background and a wild sky. Susanna stares at it, wiping her cheeks with her hands.

'It's our tree on Holne Moor,' he says gently. 'Where I proposed to you. I had to meet up with the artist, to show her photographs. Do you like it?'

And now she does cry, holding out her arms to him, as they fall together on to the bed, clutching each other tightly.

When Ed drives them under the gatehouse arch and pulls to a stop, Xander sits for a moment in silence.

'Wow,' he says softly. 'And double wow.'

Ed glances at him anxiously. 'Are you sure you're going to be OK?'

Xander nods, and they get out of the car, and

then Ed realizes that the front door is partly open, lights are on, and festive music is playing.

'Come on,' says Ed, puzzled.

He takes Xander's arm, pushes the door wide open and they go inside. The hall is full of noise and merriment. Hal and Freddie have brought in the Christmas tree. It stands tall in the corner, whilst Fliss, watching them, is holding the fairy lights in her hands, and Lulu and Ollie kneel before the boxes that contain the decorations. A log fire is burning in the huge hearth.

'Oh my God,' says Xander softly, beginning to smile.

Hal sees them and calls out. 'Good timing. Two more pairs of hands,' and suddenly everyone is laughing, talking, introducing themselves, and Ed is filled with a huge sense of gratitude and happiness. It's as if he's coming home for the first time. Xander is already part of the busy group. He turns to glance at Ed with a look of love and Ed joins them and all is well.

Freddie, seeing the look that passes between them, smiles to himself. He has his own reason to be cheerful. His latest letter from Chi-Meur was not from Sister Emily but from Clem.

> . . . This is a cry for help, old friend. The retreat house is really doing well, but our parish is going into an interregnum just after Christmas and there will be no priest to assist me. Is there any chance you could come and help us? Bed and board, of course, and a small salary, but we'd all love to have you here and it would be saving my life . . .

Freddie's heart leaped with joy and gladness. His prayers were being answered. Now he looks around the hall. Ollie is already friends with

Xander and showing him the decorations, and Lulu looks so content. Mark has tested positive for Covid and can't leave the Netherlands, and for the moment the problem of his visit is shelved. Freddie gives thanks, and murmurs the prayer his great-uncle Theo always said at family gatherings: 'God bless us, every one.'

Ed stands at his bedroom window, looking down into the courtyard. He's watching Freddie and Lulu playing a ball game with Ollie when Xander's car appears under the arch of the gatehouse and they all go to greet him as he gets out. The gatehouse lights twinkle in the dusk and Ed can't wait for him and Xander to be there together, once Freddie has gone to be chaplain at Chi-Meur. The group in the courtyard are laughing as Xander bends to catch the ball that Ollie throws to him and Ed's heart is filled with happiness. He remembers driving in, a couple of months ago, looking around him, thinking: nothing has changed. Ed turns away from the window and goes down to join the party in the courtyard.

Everything has changed.

GHOSTS

I saw her again today. I watched from an upper window whilst she paced the lawn below me and gazed up at the house. I don't recognize her. And her clothes are odd. Unfamiliar. She is not one of my band of silent friends, that is certain.

I called them that when I was a child. I was born in this house and it is in my blood and bones. I shall never leave it again. I can't remember how young I was when I became aware of my silent friends. Of course, everyone knows that the house is haunted. Why not? It is over four hundred years old, a tiny, perfect, early Elizabethan manor house. In all that time there have been enough tragedies, dramas, powerful emotions spent to leave reminders. They never frightened me. And many of them are so young. There is a small pot-boy, beaten to death by an evil-tempered groom for frightening a horse; a toddler, drowned in its bath by a drunken nanny; a young mother who died in childbed, a gag in her mouth to stifle her terrified screams lest they should waken her tyrant of a husband. There are others. They shared my childhood with me. It amazed me that no one else should be able to see them as clearly as I did. Once or twice, guests would complain of disturbed nights, movements of cold air, etc., etc., but only after they had heard the stories with their after-dinner coffee and brandy. I remember a very young child, scarcely more than a baby, strapped in its pram, its eyes following the movements of the young Victorian kitchen maid who, having found herself pregnant by the son of the house, hanged herself from a beam in the stables. And there was the teenage girl who could never sit on one of the benches placed – unknowingly – on the spot where a young Regency buck had been stabbed to death by a rival during a ball. I took her to other places in the house to see her reaction, but that was the only one that seemed to affect her. Perhaps because the young man was so young and handsome.

It broke my heart when we had to leave the house. My father had lost all his money – I never knew how – and there was talk of mortgages, repossession and the bank. It was 1930 and I was fifteen. It's a difficult age for a girl and I behaved badly. In despair, my parents summoned the doctor. But old Dr Baring had been called away and the new young doctor came in his stead. My mother was not happy about that. I could see her difficulty. It's one thing discussing certain symptoms with the elderly doctor that brought your daughter into the world, another to do so with a young, strange and very good-looking man, doctor though he may be. I fell passionately in love with him at once and the thought of leaving the house became even more intolerable. He was very kind to me. After all, he could have been barely twenty-five and probably remembered the agonies of calf love. He talked to me for a long time and put it into my head that, one day, I might come back again.

'When you are grown up,' he said, smiling at me – oh, that smile! – 'you can buy the house yourself. Or rent it.'

'How?' I cried, eagerly. 'How could I do that? I have no money.'

'Ah,' he said at once. 'Then you must earn it. Or you must marry it.'

'Marry it.' I repeated his words slowly. Such ideas were new to me.

'Yes,' he said gaily. 'You must marry a rich, handsome young man with plenty of money and persuade him to buy your home back for you.'

I did exactly that.

I met Ralph at the beginning of the war. He was a young Guards officer and had all the right qualifications. My story touched his heart. I described to him the years of our living as my uncle's pensioners, my efforts to find and keep jobs to help swell the family income. Dear Ralph. Our backgrounds were the same and he felt for me keenly. The thought of being plunged from wealth and ease to poverty and humiliation, especially for a young girl, was horrifying to him. How kind he was. How susceptible.

Through those ten long years I had watched the house. From a distance, of course, through friends, locals, the tenants themselves. Someone bought it but it wasn't long before it was back on the market. I wasn't surprised. The house was mine. I imagined my band of silent friends, custodians, guardians of my home, waiting for me to return. And so I did.

Ralph was enchanted with the place. How well I remember my return. We left the car at the gates and walked up. We were in luck. The last owner, a retired tea-planter, had been a painstaking and conscientious occupier. He had also been rich. Everything was spick and span. No peeling paint, sagging gates or waist-high grass. All was in order. The house stood in the evening sunlight, welcoming, perfect. We wandered on the terrace, over the lawns and from room to room. I was home at last. I could barely contain myself until contracts were exchanged.

'I think you'd like to camp on the lawn, my darling,' Ralph teased me. And so I would. I couldn't bear to let the house out of my sight ever again.

We had hardly moved in when Ralph was posted overseas. It seems like yesterday.

I saw her again this afternoon, pacing the terrace in the sun. Who can she be? Does she imagine that the house is empty? Soon I shall have to confront her. People have always been drawn to the house, regaled by the stories told to them at the pub in the village. I can imagine her, eyes wide, lips parted, drinking it all in. How well I know those stories, much embellished and embroidered, but with their roots buried in the truth, the most recent being that of the young wife, murdered whilst she was alone in the house one summer afternoon. They will tell her, in the pub, how the jealous husband, suspecting infidelity, came home secretly and watched her with her lover, the local doctor. Yes, that very same young man who told me how to regain my home. The husband waited for him to go and then confronted his wife, who laughed at him and told him that she wanted a divorce. Mad with grief and jealousy, he struck at her and killed her.

'Did nothing nice ever happen here?' Ralph would cry when I recounted the stories to him, during his leaves, sitting on the terrace with our drinks in the long summer evenings. 'No happy things?'

She has been here again. She came up close to the house and, approaching the french windows, peered into the drawing-room, her hands cupped round her eyes. I could bear it no longer. I loomed at her out of the shadows, suddenly, and I saw her see me, the mouth stretched in a silent shriek, the eyes wide with sudden terror. So. She has heard the stories and will not return. She will hurry back to the village to tell the news and I shall be left alone. And that is how it should be. The house is mine. I was born here and I was murdered here. Poor Ralph. So susceptible. He never saw that all I wanted was the house. And, of course, the doctor. But most of all the house, my home, now and for ever.

THE COLONIALS

When I met the Baxters I didn't realize that he was Canadian and she was American. I was introduced to Alex at a cocktail party on board the submarine. He'd just joined as the engineer officer. My husband, Philip, was first lieutenant.

'This is Alex,' someone said. 'Don't you love the pretty green uniform? He's a colonial.'

We all joined in the laughter, including Alex. After all, the Navy has names for everyone. People in the RAF are called crabs; army officers, pongos; the Fleet Air Arm, fly boys. He was a very attractive man with brown eyes, brown hair, brown skin and very white teeth. I asked if he was American.

'I certainly am not,' he said hotly. 'I'm a Canadian.' He paused. 'My wife's a Yank, though.' Sensing that I had blundered, I asked where she was. She hadn't yet arrived in England. She and the child would be arriving next week. Would I like to see the photographs? There were an awful lot of them: Alicia, his wife; JJ, his son; his home; his holiday cottage; his car. He was sweet – so proud of Alicia and JJ and so longing for them to arrive. He continued to describe them long after he'd put the photographs away. We danced. Round and round the periscope, as is the way at submarine parties, space being limited. As we revolved, he continued to apprise me of fascinating facts such as the exact age of his car, and how far it was to the landing stage on the lake from the back door of his holiday cottage back in Canada. His enthusiasm was refreshingly un-English.

When Alicia arrived, the whole wardroom was invited to dinner. I thought it was terribly brave of her to entertain eight unknown people, but it didn't worry her a bit. She greeted us like long-lost friends and served the most amazing meal. We were all struck by the size of the house. Canadian officers on exchange have large allowances. Most of us were living in poky married quarters with dreary fittings, so we gazed wide-eyed at the Baxters' five-bedroom executive house, furnished from Habitat. They basked in our admiration and Alex opened more bottles.

The other wives didn't take to Alicia. And none of us could stand JJ. He was the ultimate spoilt brat. He wouldn't share his toys, he sulked, screamed and was generally tiresome. Alicia ignored him, and rarely reprimanded him. Eventually, the rest of the wardroom wives stopped calling. I had no children to be terrorized – Philip didn't like children – so I continued to visit her.

She was hygienic to the point of mania. I remember Alex arriving home early one day while Alicia and I were having tea in the garden. She loved the English ritual of tea. He came out through the french windows, delighted to see us. Alex was an incredibly generous man – nothing pleased him more than to offer visitors hospitality. He picked up JJ, hugging him, and came to kiss Alicia.

'Don't touch me!' she cried at once. 'You're hot and sweaty. Go take a shower, then come and talk.'

'I don't need a shower.' He was clearly hurt. 'I'm not sweaty.'

'Sure you are. It's a hot day. Right? You've hurried. Right? So you've sweated. Go take a shower.'

He went, looking embarrassed, and I made sure that I was gone before he reappeared.

Alicia spent a great deal of time – and money – buying English things to take Back Home. 'Just wait till Mom sees this!' she'd cry, showing me a set of Waterford crystal, beautiful table linen, jerseys from

Marks & Spencer. She was very close to her mother. They were always exchanging cards. The Americans have greeting cards for all occasions, and Alicia became quite distraught when she couldn't find a St Patrick's Day card to send to 'Mom'. The minute the submarine went to sea she'd be on a plane to the States. To begin with, she was always back before the boat docked. Then one day the boat got in early and Alicia wasn't there to meet it. To say that Alex was upset was putting it mildly. We tried to calm him down. After all, Alicia couldn't have known that the boat would be in early. Usually the wretched thing was late.

'That's not the point,' was all that he would say. 'If she'd stayed she'd have been here.' This was unarguable. 'Why does she rush home every time I go away? It was only for six weeks, this time. Did you rush home to mom?'

I had to admit that I had not. By this time Philip and I had persuaded him to come home with us. 'But it's different for me,' I pointed out. 'My mother is only two hours away. It's bound to be lonely for Alicia, on her own in a strange country.'

'She should want to be where I am,' he said bleakly. 'And JJ, too. I should never have married a Yank.'

Philip strolled in, looked around and picked up the newspaper. 'She'll be back in a day or two. Couldn't be *Star Trek* night, could it?' He wandered out again.

'He's gonna watch TV? His first night home for six weeks and he's gonna watch TV?' Alex shook his head. 'You English are real cool.'

'Not all of us, Alex.' We looked at each other for a long time.

When Alicia arrived back, we met for lunch.

'Gee, was he mad,' she shrugged. 'What's it matter, two or three little days? I didn't want to come back, I can tell you.'

'Most women would be delighted to have such an affectionate husband. You should be pleased.'

She shrugged again. 'He's only got one thing on his mind. He's real dirty. He likes watching me undress! Can you imagine! Like I was out of a porno magazine or something.'

'He just loves you, that's all,' I said wistfully.

She shook her head. 'I should never have married a Canuck.'

The next time she didn't come back at all. Said it wasn't worth it. He'd be going away again too soon. She'd decided to stay with Mom. So that was that. The divorce came through very quickly. I was delighted, of course.

I'm wonderfully happy in his home with our baby. And I know exactly how far it is to the landing stage on the lake from the back door of his holiday cottage.

KATH

Yesterday I saw a ghost. As I glanced casually through the window of the sales rooms, I saw her. It was Kath, staring out into the street, her face haloed by a silvery softness. Kath: my dearest friend and worst enemy. She looked exactly as she had just before she died: her eyes shadowed and watchful, her mouth strained. How different that plain, unhappy face was from the sweet-tempered Kath I'd first met at art school!

Kath had stood apart from the crowd, not a shaker or a mover, just different: she had style and talent and her own brand of elusive charm. She and I hit it off together and we remained close friends after college when I went into interior design and she got a job in an advertising agency. Kath gave great parties, thoughtfully orchestrated, with the guest list carefully balanced, and it was at one of these parties that I met Jake. Kath had already told me about Jake: she worked with him and it was obvious that she was in love with him. Everyone loved Jake: men and women alike were simply drawn to him. He was such fun: he had the knack of making anyone, however ordinary or dull, feel special. I fell in love with him, too.

Jake was recovering from the break-up of a long-standing relationship. Plenty of women were very ready to console him, me included. But when the time came for Jake to choose a new partner he chose Kath. By now I was so crazy about him that I could hardly conceal my envy. Kath was really sympathetic but she was so happy that she couldn't really connect with me. It was hell seeing them together and I avoided them as much as I could. Kath was so obsessed with Jake that she hardly noticed. I accepted a good job in Manchester and it was a relief not to see Kath and Jake too often – I still wasn't over him – but I made brief visits to see them and my other friends in London.

After a while Kath began to change. First her sense of style deserted her, then her sparkle dimmed; gradually a haunted look appeared about her eyes and she lost weight. All this happened over a period of time but I noticed the changes. I travelled down to London as soon as I heard she'd taken an overdose. I felt so guilty that she hadn't been able to talk about her problems with me, but Jake reassured me I could not have helped. She'd become withdrawn and unstable. Something to do with being unable to have a baby, he said. It was clear that things had been very difficult and I was only too willing to comfort him.

I moved in with Jake after a month or so; gave up my job in Manchester and started to freelance. God,

I was so happy! I utterly adored him – although I could never quite get Kath out of my mind. I found that she'd be there at odd moments: when Jake was late home, for instance. He'd make me laugh, describing the clients he'd been with, and then he'd make love as if it were his last night on earth. He took a great interest in what I wore and how I looked, and I sometimes felt Kath at my shoulder when he said things like: 'Is it time you got your hair trimmed? I'm not sure that style is very flattering. Bit ageing, perhaps? Laura was looking terrific yesterday, wasn't she?' Or 'Are you going to wear that short skirt this evening? Not that your legs aren't great, but what did you think of Suzy's long skirt? Very sexy, actually.' Of course, I knew that it was only because he cared, wanted me to look my best, but when we went to parties I'd catch myself watching him to see who he was admiring. I wondered if Kath had done the same.

I began to lose confidence in my own taste. Jake was such a star that it was difficult to sparkle with equal brilliance within his orbit and I got used to taking a back seat. I didn't mind at first. It was enough to be his partner, the one he'd chosen. Women were always jostling for my place and he was incapable of being unkind to them. Once, though, when I accused him of leading one of them on, he reacted coolly. His expression was a mixture of disappointment and a chilly scrutiny, which made me nervous. I felt that it was I who was to blame for being small-minded and jealous, and that I had let him down in some way. I became more careful and tried not to act foolishly although there were often phone messages from women who clearly believed that he was available. I was humiliated but I never dared let him see it. Somehow he always managed to make me feel that it was my fault: that I was becoming paranoid and unbalanced.

Gradually the effect of this was that I began to feel exhausted, as if life were increasingly an intolerable strain, and I stopped accompanying him quite so regularly on the endless round of parties and entertainments. I spent evenings alone, trying not to imagine Jake surrounded by adoring women. But I couldn't quite control my fear. The situation got worse, my suspicions were less easily subjugated, and I became very unhappy. That's how it was that morning, out shopping, when I found myself thinking about Kath.

Of course it wasn't her ghost I saw. After I'd recovered from the shock I went back and looked through the window again. It was my own face, reflected in a huge looking-glass hanging on the back wall of the shop, but the haunted eyes and unhappy mouth might have been hers. I was shocked. I telephoned my former boss in Manchester and asked if I could come back. She offered me my old job and, by the time Jake came home, I was packed and ready to leave. He didn't say too much, and neither of us mentioned Kath, but I felt very close to her. I think she saved my life.

ELIZABETH DRAKE

I saw a rook today with a straw in its beak and, all at once, I was back in the past, hearing Elizabeth Drake saying, 'I love the spring. New life, rebirth. I'm an Easter person.'

Elizabeth Drake. I can picture her quite clearly. I thought her old but she was probably no more than thirty-eight. She was very fastidious: her shirts, plain and simple, were always immaculate; her skirts, practical, newly pressed; her shoes, sensible, highly polished. She wore the minimum amount of make-up and her short, dark hair was always in place. I could never imagine her being passionate, frantic. At least, not in the beginning.

She was my boss, the manager and buyer of the department and the only member of staff who treated me as an ordinary person and not as a friend of the chairman's son. I don't know how the others knew – I never mentioned it – but they knew; everyone was charming to me. Soon I realized that they all hated Elizabeth Drake. Looking back, I think she committed the cardinal sin of letting them see that she felt herself superior to them. Well, so she was.

Mrs Steed. I can see her, too: fair, fat and forty, dressed to kill and with a bubbly charm that disguised the thinness of the brightly painted lips and the calculating coldness in the pale blue eyes. This is with hindsight: at the time I was flattered by her friendliness. She helped out with anyone who was short-staffed, strutting between departments on high-heeled shoes, her ample bottom tightly encased in short skirts chosen to display plump calves in shiny stockings. She was very popular with the men and livened up the atmosphere of the dismal canteen.

Elizabeth Drake always went out to lunch. Brisk, looking neither to right nor left, pulling on her gloves, she would leave the department, descend the stairs and vanish into the throng beyond the glass doors. Once she'd gone, one or two of the staff would gather together and the whispering would begin. In the early days I was left well alone. Perhaps no one quite knew whose side I would take and what I might say to a higher authority. The chief whisperers were Mr Basset from Carpets, Mrs Steed, and Mr Griffiths: the manager and buyer of Soft Furnishings. He had a peculiarly menacing smile, I remember: he never opened his lips. His silvery hair was plastered to his skull and he always wore a pinstriped suit.

He asked me questions about the department: how were our sales figures for the month, our budget and so on. When Elizabeth Drake found out she was furious.

'And I suppose you tell him everything,' she exclaimed bitterly.

By this time I was used to her antagonism to the staff and her dislike of my friendly overtures towards them, but I was irked by the feeling of 'them and us'; that our department was an oasis amidst the infidel. I was young, light-hearted and I wanted to laugh with Griff and Mr Basset, gossip with Mrs Steed. They'd appear the moment she left at lunchtime.

'Where's the gorgon?' they'd ask. 'Gone to Mass?'

It was the first I'd heard of Elizabeth Drake being a Roman Catholic, and I recalled a conversation we'd had about abortion and how unusually heated she'd become. It was about the same time that I'd told her how much I loved the autumn: the colours, the wood smoke and the anticipation of Christmas.

'Oh, no,' she said. 'I hate the autumn. Dank and

cheerless, dark nights and winter ahead. So depressing. I love the spring, new life, rebirth. I'm an Easter person. Wait till you're older; you'll feel as I do.'

'But Christmas,' I pressed her. 'Surely you like Christmas?'

Her face closed. 'I hate Christmas,' she said. And that was that.

Time passed and my birthday arrived. She gave me a little leather-bound book of Shakespeare's Sonnets. On the flyleaf she'd inscribed a quote about friendship and values. I can't for the life of me remember it now and I've lost the book. At the time I was more excited by Mrs Steed's present of a silk scarf.

As the time approached for Elizabeth Drake to take her holiday she became agitated.

'I asked the MD to let me leave you in charge,' she said, 'but he says you haven't enough experience. Mrs Steed's going to be here with you.'

I opened my mouth to say, 'What fun!' and shut it

again. She spent all day putting things away, locking drawers and leaving me with endless dos and don'ts. Mrs Steed came into the department during the afternoon to see if there were any instructions for her. Dislike crackled tangibly beneath their icy politeness and I could see, just round the corner, Griff rubbing his hands and smiling to himself.

The next two weeks were carnival. Mrs Steed's friends dropped in and other members of staff stopped by for little chats. When Elizabeth Drake returned it was like being back at school after the holidays. She went through the department from top to bottom, then settled down to check the figures. Members of staff gave me little winks and nods of sympathy and I felt that, imperceptibly, I had moved from her side to theirs. She set me to change the department round, no doubt to throw off any lingering memory of Mrs Steed, and I was hard at it all day.

'Shame,' whispered Mrs Steed. 'Miserable old cow. We had such fun, didn't we?'

'Shame,' whispered Griff. 'Pity she didn't drown on her holiday. Janice Steed should run your department.'

Things didn't improve and when I heard of a job at the local antiques shop I applied for it and got it. I went at once to the MD's office to give in my notice. He looked tired and worried, his fingers pressing constantly just above his waistline. On his desk stood a glass of milk.

'I wonder, Miss Beauchamp, if you've given it long enough,' he said. 'I can understand that it's not too exciting for a young person of your age, but soon you'll be learning how to buy . . .'

At last I said, 'To be honest I really don't want to work with Mrs Drake any more. We're not compatible.'

He sat up straight then. 'Well, if that's the case Mrs Steed can run the department. You get on very well with her, don't you?'

I stared at him. 'Yes, but that's not the point . . .'

'Don't worry, my dear.' He stood up and came round the desk. 'She'll be no loss, I assure you.'

'You don't understand,' I began, but he was escorting me out of the door.

When Elizabeth Drake appeared in the department later, I tried to hide. She seized me by the arm, her face blotched and her mouth stretched into an ugly shape.

'Why did you do this?' she cried. 'We've got on very well. Why did you say you couldn't work with me?'

'I didn't.' I tried to free myself, shocked by her appearance. 'I didn't actually say that. I'm leaving anyway. It's nothing to do with you.'

'Will you say that? Will you come with me now and say that?' She was dragging me towards the stairs, oblivious of the interested stares. I was hot with shame and embarrassment. I knew that I had done something dreadful.

'Please,' I begged her, 'please wait. I will go. Be calm.' But she wouldn't listen. Mr Harrigan, the assistant manager was coming down the stairs and she flew at him, dragging me with her.

'Miss Beauchamp says that it's nothing to do with me,' she cried to him. 'She's prepared to go now and say so. It's all a mistake. Please . . .'

It was dreadful. I wondered how on earth she could contemplate continuing to work there having exposed herself so completely to her enemies. Mr Harrigan hustled her away and presently reappeared to suggest that I should go to lunch. When I came back she'd gone. No sign of her was left behind and in her place was Mrs Steed, triumphant at last. The place was agog. Rumours raced round the departments.

'White as a sheet she was when she left,' reported Griff, smiling. 'I watched her. She passed right by me.' How he would have enjoyed it.

'So that's that,' Mrs Steed could barely hide her exaltation. How well I had played her cards for her. 'Let's tidy up a bit, shall we?'

I left anyway. I went to say goodbye to Mr Harrigan. He was a gentle, quiet man with a limp and had been patently distressed by the scene on the stairs. I told him how sorry I was, how it had all been a bit of a muddle. It made me feel slightly better to say that . . . Less guilty.

'Poor woman.' He shook his head. His mild gaze roamed the middle distance. 'Such a tragic story. Her husband is an invalid, you know. He was knocked down by a drunken driver one Christmas Eve. The child was killed.'

'Child?'

His gaze returned to me. 'I shouldn't have mentioned it but she's gone and you're going, too. Don't tell anyone else, please.'

I said again, 'Child?'

He sighed. 'She had a child. He was two or three, I think. After the accident it was found that her husband would never be able to provide her with another. It was a dreadful grief to her. She has to work to support him, now.'

I searched for her for weeks but with no luck. Time passed and I got married. Some years later, as I was pushing my second child through the China and Glass department of a large store, I saw her. I watched her for a while and then went up to her.

'Hello,' I said. After a moment she smiled, coolly, warily.

'I looked for you,' I said. 'I wanted to apologize. Can you ever forgive me?'

'I'll try,' she said. And then she saw Archie. 'You have a child,' she said, and came right round the counter to look at him. I felt my throat constrict.

'Two, actually,' I said. She crouched beside him and he stared at her stolidly, thumb in mouth. She looked up at me. 'I have a son, too,' she said – and her face blazed with love and pride. I stared. She touched Archie's cheek with her finger and stood up.

'I couldn't get another job, you see, so we decided to adopt. You get all sorts of help and allowances. He's started school, now, so I'm working part time.' Her smile, this time, was warmer. 'I forgave you long ago, actually. When Andrew arrived.'

I nodded: words were difficult. 'So you don't hate Christmas any more?'

'Not any more. But I still like spring best.'

I never saw her again but it all came back to me when I saw the rook with the straw in his beak.

I wish I could find that book of Shakespeare's Sonnets, though.

THE HAWK

Each morning, between washing and dressing, she sits on the window seat watching the birds. Her bedroom window looks out on to a small square lawn edged with deep borders and surrounded by a dry-stone wall. Now, in February, there is a sense of new life beginning: the burning blue flowers of *Iris stylosa* can be seen behind the decaying chrysanthemums, whilst the *Helleborus orientalis* – the Lenten rose – blooms in the shelter of the wall. In the centre of the grass stands the bird table beside the stump of an old tree. There are breadcrumbs on the table and a container holding nuts hangs from a nail next to a chunk of suet secured with twine. Whilst her mother prepares breakfast downstairs in the large, warm farmhouse kitchen, and her younger brother and sisters play noisily in the adjoining bedrooms, she sits, huddled in an old dressing gown, anthropomorphizing.

The jaunty sparrows and the saucy blue tits are the younger children in this society. They jostle and push good humouredly, getting in each other's way, enjoying themselves, confident that the food will always be here and that there will always be enough. A robin with one white feather in his wing hovers on the edge of the mêlée, dashing in to seize a crumb, but easily frightened away. This is the character with which she identifies most closely.

Greenfinches are the adolescents: preening, outwardly confident, yet fearing that there will always be a rival and that you must be prepared to fight for what you want. They open their beaks at one another and chase each other away from the food. The handsome great tits, vividly marked with black and yellow, are the adults of the group: self-assured and in control, rarely having to exert their authority over the smaller species.

The starlings, brash and ruthlessly opportunist, are the chancers of this community. Even now, as she watches, they swoop down from the tall oak at the end of the garden, scattering all and sundry to settle on the table, squabbling noisily over the food, eating fast and greedily.

She bangs angrily on the window, flinging it open, and they fly away, only to gather again – sullen but watchful, she feels – at the top of the tree, waiting for the next chance. The other birds, strangely, are unperturbed by her banging and return almost immediately to the food so as to make good use of the time before the starlings descend again, as they surely will. After a moment they do. It is a cold morning and they are hungry. Down they come in a swirling cloud and again the smaller birds are driven off. Before she can chase them away, a speck that has been circling high above now drops suddenly earthwards. Instantly, in a flashing kaleidoscope of feathers, the grassy square is deserted, and here, sitting on the tree stump, is the sparrowhawk. Golden-eyed, it broods over the empty scene, its needle-sharp talons gripping the rotting wood. Even with the rounded, bright grey wings folded, it looks dangerous and exciting; its power is palpable even in repose. Presently it shifts, balancing carefully on long yellow legs before lifting into the airy spaces above the fields and woodland.

Her mother's voice calling crossly up the stairs brings her back to the present. Hastily she dresses, pulling on the drab uniform and wishing that she had that flair with which some of the other girls transform these unflattering garments. Even if she had the knack of turning herself from ugly duckling into swan, she knows that her mother would disapprove, just as she disapproves of the new coffee bar in the town and the pop music that is played on its jukebox. As she finishes dressing, pausing to stare at herself in the small, age-spotted glass that stands on the chest of drawers, she sighs regretfully, experimentally pulling a few feathery tendrils around her small face. She wishes that she was dark and glamorous, despising her flax-fair hair and the pale skin, which colours so readily when she is anxious. As she hurries downstairs she calls to the younger ones, telling them to get a move on.

She drops her satchel at the kitchen door and slides into her place, her eyes searching the pile of letters at the other end of the old pine table.

'Anything for me?'

'Why should there be?' Her mother, thin, harassed, tired from being up most of the night in the lambing pens, dumps a plate of porridge in front of her eldest daughter. There are two younger girls upstairs, and a son, with whom she must wrestle and get organized for the walk to the village school. 'If you didn't daydream all morning you could help with the others. Time you began to think about other people.' This brief homily successfully disguises the huge pride that she has in her child's achievement: a scholarship to the prestigious High School in the large town ten miles away.

'Sorry, Mum.' She sighs inwardly and attacks the porridge; it's always the same, every morning, but she feels the need to justify herself. 'You know they won't do anything I say and then they make me late. It's all right for them, they don't have to catch the bus.'

'Don't whine. And get a move on or you won't be catching the bus either.'

Ten minutes later she is walking up the track. The frozen mud, shaped into patterns by tractor wheels, feels lumpy beneath her feet, the splintered ice glazing the rutted puddles. When she reaches the lane she stares out across the hills; the familiar landscape is transformed by the powdery dusting of frost, mysterious and magical. The bus approaches, wheezing and coughing up the hill, pulls alongside her and she climbs in.

The driver, in his black and yellow jacket, reminds her of the great tit: large, assured. He nods to her as she shows him her school pass and the bus lurches forward as she makes her way down the swaying aisle; past a businessman, soberly clad as any rook, engrossed in his newspaper; past a matronly, cheerful-looking woman, comfortable and content as a pigeon, her shopping basket resting on her ample knees; past the younger schoolchildren, squabbling and twittering together.

The back seats are usually occupied by the older boys from the Grammar School: starling-like, they are a confident, swaggering group who, in the main, ignore her. Occasionally they tease her just to see her blush, but they are more interested in the older, more sophisticated girls: the greenfinches, preening and giggling together, huddled in their seats, watching jealously lest the boys should pay more attention to one girl than to another, but displaying an outward show of solidarity.

'Hello, Sarah. Get any Valentine cards?' The speaker, a girl, is nudged by her companion and they burst into a fit of giggles.

She has made a few good friends at school, none of whom catch this bus, but she has not yet mastered the easy repartee with which to defend herself against the teasing, so she looks out of the window, her cheeks red, and tries to pretend she cannot hear the bantering that follows the question. The bus stops, starts up again, and she is aware of a little silence, a few whispers. Up the aisle towards her strolls the head boy of the Grammar School: captain of cricket, captain of the first eleven and with a place at Oxford, conditional on exam results, of course, but no one doubts he'll make it. He rarely catches the bus and the girls are caught off balance, smoothing sleek hair, trying to catch his eye. The starlings are silent at the back, showing respect for his superior agile strength and predatory glance. He sprinkles a smile here, a nod there – and sits beside her. She feels enormous in her bulky coat, clumsy, a stereotypical farmer's daughter, and stares determinedly, if unseeingly, out of the window.

'Hello.'

Can he possibly be speaking to her? She darts a glance at him. He is. She swallows in a dry throat, the treacherous scarlet blazing in her cheeks, and manages to answer.

'Hello.'

The girls' High School and the boys' Grammar School join together for various events and she has worshipped him from afar for many months: he is her hero, her god, her hawk. He smiles, sitting poised and proud in his seat, rather as the sparrowhawk sat on the stump, looking at them all; those lesser species. Her heart trembles and flutters in her side as she feels the warmth of his arm pressed against her own; she is aware of an odd, stomach-churning weakness as she sees his long fingers relaxed upon his grey flannel knee.

'Coming to the theatre on Saturday?'

She looks at him. There is to be a matinée performance of *The Merchant of Venice* to which some of the senior classes are being taken.

'Oh.' Her palms are wet and surely he can hear the beating of her blood. 'Yes. Yes, I am.'

'Good!' His eyes are golden like the sparrowhawk's, ringed with black. 'See you there, then. And you don't have to rush off afterwards, you know. Why not stay? We could go for a cup of coffee in the town. Would you like that?'

'I don't know. I hadn't thought.'

'Well. Why not think about it now?'

They've reached the bus station and their fellow

students are leaping up, dragging satchels and bags from the racks, fighting to be first out.

'Oh, by the way.' He's on his feet, bending over her, screening her from the curious eyes of the greenfinches and starlings who are filing past. 'This is for you. Better look at it later.'

He hefts his grip lightly from the rack and is gone. She hesitates, turning the envelope in her hand, and presently, when the bus is quite empty, has a surreptitious peep. It is a Valentine card. On it is the picture of a knight in full armour seated on the back of a huge shaggy dog, with rain pouring down upon them, and inside the words: 'Surely you wouldn't turn away a knight on a dog like this?'

She stands up, thrusting the card into her pocket, her eyes shining.

'Decided to play truant today, then?' The bus driver is standing on the steps, waiting for her.

'Sorry.' She seizes her satchel and hurries down the bus towards him. 'Sorry. Lost something.'

'Well, by the look on your face I should think you've found it, eh?'

'Yes. Yes, I have.' She climbs off the bus, smiles back at him.

It is the happiest day of her life.

SMOKE SCREEN

Francesca had those long, very slim legs with elegant ankles that look so wonderful in black silk: she also had a handsome, successful husband, four delightful children, a beautiful house, and she loved to show them off.

'Come to lunch,' she'd cry down the telephone. 'Stay to tea. Do come. Sundays are so deadly on your own.'

Sometimes I'd go. It was as if a huge play were being enacted for my entertainment. The family would be waiting for me: four-year-old twins, Sophie and Lucy, six-year-old Henry, and Francesca with the baby in her arms. Then Tom would make his appearance, dead on cue, strolling out of the front door with a bottle in his hands and calling to his offspring.

'For goodness' sake! Put her down! Put her down!'

He'd nuzzle my neck, telling me how ravishing I looked, whilst Francesca smiled tolerantly, glad to see me enjoying these few crumbs from the rich man's table. I've no doubt she thought I fancied him but, frankly, I was more interested in his cellar.

Sometimes it was drinks in the garden and a barbecue. Sometimes we'd eat at the huge kitchen table – crusty bread, home-made soup, really good cheese. Sometimes, if there were other guests, it would be a pukka lunch in the lofty, well-proportioned dining-room. I enjoyed myself. Of course I did. The play doesn't cease to entertain merely because one can occasionally see the trappings. On those days that there were other guests I was the only one who stayed on beyond tea.

'After all,' Francesca would say, 'you haven't got anything else to do, have you?' By then I wanted very much to go home to my quiet little house, but some pleasure would have gone from Francesca's day if I'd suggested this. Back we'd go into the house to the ritual of bathtime and bedtime.

I was delegated storyteller; the children, scrubbed and sweet-smelling, posed prettily. I'd read them one story each, my tongue hanging out for a drink, then hurry downstairs to tell Tom that they were waiting to say goodnight.

'Here's your drink,' he'd say, 'just as you like it.'

I'd have a few quiet moments, wondering what was for supper, and then they'd come in together exuding a mixture of self-satisfaction, achievement and exhaustion.

'Honestly!' Francesca would slump into a chair. 'Why do we have kids!'

It was at one of these Sunday lunches that I first met Jenny and Rob. Jenny was short and round, pretty enough and very gentle; the children adored her. Rob was good-looking and sweet tempered. Tom now had another female to make up to. His harem – that's what he called us.

'All these women,' he'd cry. 'I love 'em all.'

Francesca had no qualms: Jenny and I were like a pair of Dartmoor ponies alongside a thoroughbred. It was all good fun.

I can't put my finger on the moment that things began to change. It was too nebulous, too subtle. Tom and Rob spent a lot of time together. They both loved fishing and occasionally went off for a fishing weekend. Francesca would invite Jenny over and they'd have a great time together. Perhaps it was the holiday that brought things to a head. Tom and Francesca were off to a villa in Tuscany.

'Guess what!' said Francesca. 'Tom wants to invite Jenny and Rob to go with us.'

I was surprised – holidays were the one thing they did alone as a family – but I shrugged.

'Perhaps he thinks it would be nice for you to have help with the children. Jenny's terrific with the kids and Sam is very small.'

'Mm. He never worried about that when the others were little.'

'I expect he wants you to enjoy yourself, perhaps have a little time with him on your own. Rob and Jenny can babysit. Surely you can't imagine that he has an ulterior motive? I can't see Jenny cutting you out once you both get into bikinis.'

She laughed at that. 'He pays a lot of attention to her, though,' she said, brow wrinkling.

'So he does to me. It's Tom's way. What's got into you?'

'I don't know. I seem to have some sort of presentiment of doom.'

'Time of the month, I should think. What about that drink you promised me.'

But she was right. After the holiday I began to notice a certain tension during our Sundays together. Tom was paying a lot of attention to Jenny whilst Rob seemed quieter than ever. I caught him looking at Tom with a very strange expression. However, they went off together for a shooting weekend although Jenny didn't stay with Francesca as she usually did on these occasions.

Some time passed before I went over to Sunday lunch. It was more formal, this time, with quite a lot of guests. Tom flirted with all the women, but there was an air of strain in his performance. Rob spent most of the time with Henry, building a model plane, and this time it was Jenny who watched Tom, staring with great anguished eyes as he put his arms round the women, nuzzling at their necks and whispering to them.

I found Francesca in the kitchen, beautiful as ever. Impossible that she should lose him. She smiled at me but was too surrounded by people to talk. As I went back into the hall I saw a flash of white through a half-open door. Tom held the inevitable bottle in one hand whilst Rob grasped him by the arms. He seemed to be remonstrating with him and his face had a beseeching look. Tom shook him off and I slipped away. Rob and Jenny left early that day and there were tears on Jenny's cheeks.

A few weeks later Francesca telephoned. 'He's gone.' Her voice was barely audible through her tears. 'They've gone away together. Can you imagine . . . ?' I went straight over.

I don't know what happened to Jenny but Francesca's world was reduced to rubble. I wonder if there were clues that I missed; whether through unconscious prejudice I chose to ignore Rob and Tom's relationship. I don't think so. Sometimes the truth defeats even the most sharp-eyed of us, especially when it's unexpected.

DAISY MILLER

The first time I heard the name Daisy Miller was on a warm afternoon at the beginning of June. In the small fishing town, where grey stone houses clung to the steep cobbled streets, the very walls were bursting into bloom: red valerian sprang from tiny crevices alongside clumps of feverfew. In the network of deep, secret lanes beyond the village, honeysuckle scrambled through the hedges where the pale flowers of the dog rose blossomed on thorny trailing stems.

I'd taken five-year-old Robby to school, walking

with him down the steps of narrow alleys towards the quay, planning to do some shopping afterwards. It was nearly a year since Ben and I sold our small London flat and moved westwards. To begin with it hadn't been easy but now he was getting lots of photographic assignments and was signed up to do two major tourist brochures. My own work – local scenes done in pastels and sold as cards or small paintings – had attracted some interest and now, with Robby at school, I had more time to spend on developing a network of retail outlets.

When I realized that I'd forgotten my purse I cursed under my breath and made my way back to the cottage. It was a very small one, perched on the corner of two alleys with a glimpse of the sea between the high walls, but it had an attic, which I used as a workroom, and a delightfully private courtyard where the sun slanted in and a wild mallow grew. Ben rented a lock-up shop and dark-room a few streets away in the town, although he came home most days for lunch, so I wasn't particularly surprised to hear his voice when I let myself in.

I don't quite know why I didn't immediately shout to him – he knew I was planning to do some shopping and he wasn't prepared for me to be back so soon – but, even as I opened my mouth to call, something prevented me. He was up in the slip of a room that we jokingly called the library, because it was shelved from ceiling to floor and held most of our book collection. There was just enough space for a very small table with the telephone on it and a chair.

It was the tone of his voice that alerted me: it held excitement – and amusement. All my instincts were alerted and I stood quite still inside the door, listening.

'Sounds perfect . . . I should like that very much . . . Sorry, who did you say? . . . Daisy Miller? Oh, yes, I see' – a little burst of laughter – 'Brilliant! . . . Looking forward to it.'

As he came out to the top of the stairs I caught a

glimpse of his expression: alive, excited, secretive. It was gone in a flash and he stared down at me, disconcerted.

'Hi,' I said easily, though my heart was thumping at his look, which lent confirmation to my fears. 'Forgot my purse.'

'Right.' He came on down, clearly trying to hide his anxiety. 'I was just calling a client.'

I nodded. I didn't query it; I didn't say casually, 'But you never make business calls from home. It's one of your rules,' because I was already too frightened to confront him. His guilty look, combined with the words I'd overheard, seemed to clamp my tongue. I felt stiff and awkward and he hesitated for a moment, said, 'See you later, then,' and went out quickly.

I told myself not to be a fool, found my purse, but then I went upstairs and looked into the library. A sheet of paper had been roughly torn from the pad, nothing more. Later he telephoned.

'Shan't be in for lunch,' he said. 'Out on a job. See you later on.'

As the days passed my fears grew: Ben was preoccupied, yet he was clearly suppressing some kind of excitement. Twice he telephoned to say he couldn't get home and he seemed to be working even harder than usual.

Then, one day I went into his office knowing that he was away. He couldn't afford an assistant yet and I had a key in case of emergencies. Feeling ashamed but desperate, I checked through the papers on his desk. Clipped into a notebook was the sheet torn from the pad. There was a telephone number written at the top and, underneath the name: Daisy Miller. After a long moment I dialled the number.

'Hello,' I said. 'Is that . . . could I speak to Daisy Miller, please?'

'She's out,' the voice said cheerfully. 'Meeting someone, she said. Can I ask her to call you back?'

'No,' I answered quickly, 'I'll try some other time.'

As I stood there I imagined her, this Daisy Miller: elegant, pretty, with long fair hair and tremendous charm.

When Ben got home much later, he was still in that strange mood of high exaltation. I felt miserable, knowing that I must speak to him, confront my fear, but deciding to wait until after my birthday. Ben had suggested no plans but the afternoon before the day itself he came home unexpectedly early.

'I've got something to show you,' he said. 'Come on.'

I followed him down to the harbour and along the wall. A small sailing boat, brightly varnished, bobbed at her mooring. As she swung with the tide I saw the name painted on her transom: *Daisy Miller.*

'I know how much you've longed for a boat,' Ben was saying. 'She was built for a lady called Daisy Miller when she was a girl. She's too old to manage her any longer so I've bought her for you. I've taken on some extra work so we can just about afford it . . .'

He was taken aback but pleased by my reaction: overwhelming joy, relief, gratitude . . . and shame.

That happened years ago and now my grandchildren sail her whenever they can; but *Daisy Miller* taught me a lesson about trust that I've never forgotten.

ACKNOWLEDGEMENTS

First and foremost, to my much-loved late husband Roddy, who persuaded me to write and thus to make me the following friends:

Cate Paterson, Clare Foss, the late Jane Morpeth, Yvonne Holland, Sue Fletcher, Susie Watts, Linda Evans, Patrick Janson-Smith, Larry Finlay, Bill Scott-Kerr, Kevin Redmond, Harriet Bourton, Francesca Best, Molly Crawford, Imogen Nelson, Vivien Thompson, Josh Benn, Marianne Issa El-Khoury, Helen Edwards, Chris Smale, Tom Hill, Hayley Barnes, Izzie

Ghaffari-Parker, Josh Crosley, Kiran Kataria, Fay Pafford, Kathleen Anderson, Tom Dunne, Marcia Markland, Hilary McMahon, Kim McArthur, Regina Hartig, Iris Gehrman, Christian Stuewe, Ulf Töregård, Ninni Töregård, Alis Friis Caspersen, Niels Gudbergsen, Anne Sondergaard, Elisabeth Strandgaard, Trine Maehl, Frederika von Traa, Karen Bikkel, Michelle Lapautre, Catherine Lapautre, Claire de Robespierre, Krista Kaer, Nike Davarinou, Louisa Zaoussi, Jill Hughes.

I would like to thank the illustrators of my books all over the world whose beautiful cover designs have given me so much joy.

I am very grateful to Bob Mann who gave me my first press review, to Annette Shaw at *Devon Life*, to Judi Spiers and all at Radio Devon. To Pat Abrehardt who arranged my very first signing party, and to all staff at the Harbour Bookshop in Kingsbridge. To Simon and Natasha at Bookstop, to Cliff and Martin at Totnes Bookshop, to Andrea at the Community Bookshop and the staff at Browser Bookshop in Dartmouth, as well as other local booksellers who have stocked and sold so many copies of my novels.

I have been constantly encouraged by messages from loyal readers, especially Marilyn Bertrand. Thank you all for your emails which have been such a joy to receive.

Love to my sisters Paula and Bridget, whose eagle eye prevented many mistakes, and to Pam Goddard, whose early read of my manuscripts was always invaluable.

Special thanks to Rick. Without your technical support and advice, it would have been very difficult for me to write my later novels.

Finally, very special thanks to my agent Dinah.

Discover more of Marica's heartwarming tales . . .

As Christmas approaches, everything seems to be falling into place for Dossie. Her son Clem and his adorable four-year-old son Jakey have moved to Cornwall to be closer to her. She runs her own successful catering business. All she needs now is for the run of bad luck in her romantic life to end . . .

But while little Jakey helps to put away the decorations after another cosy Christmas surrounded by friends and family, an avaricious property developer starts prowling around. The Cornish home which he has known all his life is in danger of being sold up, and everything is changing.

Will this close-knit unit who so depend on each other still be together next Christmas? And what will they have learnt about having somewhere you truly belong?

With unforgettable characters, charming romance and plenty of warmth, *The Christmas Angel* is the perfect Christmas read.

AVAILABLE NOW

Childhood friends and cousins Leo and Alice had imagined their whole lives playing out on their beloved Devon beach. But one night when they are teens, sitting on the sand beneath the stars, Alice tells Leo a secret that must never be shared with anybody else . . . then packs her bag and flees.

Leo is left to build his own life – without Alice. He surrounds himself with other family and friends and on the whole is content and fulfilled. But he is left with a sense of what – or who – is missing. So decades later, when he receives a note from Alice asking if she can come home, he doesn't hesitate to agree.

But as the stars align and their reunion draws near, Leo is left to consider their separation and what so many years apart means for a relationship solidified in youth and a secret which could affect the whole family.

AVAILABLE NOW

When Mattie invites her old friend Tim to stay in one of her family cottages on the edge of Dartmoor, she senses there is something he is not telling her, as if he is holding on to a painful secret.

But as he gets to know the rest of the warm jumble of family who live by the moor, Tim discovers that everyone there has their own secrets. There is Charlotte, a young navy wife struggling to bring up her son while her husband is at sea; William, who guards a dark past he cannot share with the others; and Mattie, who has loved Tim in silence for years.

As Tim begins to open up, Mattie falls deeper in love. And as summer warms the wild Dartmoor landscape, new beginnings take root . . . But can fresh hopes bloom where old secrets are buried?

AVAILABLE NOW

After her husband dies, Cara no longer wishes to live in their London home. On impulse, she sells it and goes to stay with her brother in Salcombe, Devon, while she plans her next move. There, she begins to look back at her life and reflect on the choices that have led her to this moment.

Cosmo has also escaped – temporarily – from his life in the city, finding the south-west a relaxing and appealing fit, especially when he meets local girl, Amy. But is he being entirely truthful about what he's left behind?

Just out of uni, Sam has passed the Admiralty Interview Board and is set to follow in his naval father's footsteps. His future is secure – but he feels cast adrift. With doubts and loosening family connections worrying him, an impartial new friend could be just the thing he needs. Forging a bond across the generations, can he and Cara help each other find the way to a new, happy chapter?

AVAILABLE NOW